"Mornin', ma'am," he said.

Her face came alive with recognition and a slight smile tilted her mouth. "Now I remember. You rode by last evening, didn't you?"

"Yes, ma'am." He nodded a thank-you to the man who handed him a cup.

"I didn't recognize you at first." She quickly scanned his attire and glanced away.

Caleb rubbed his jawline. "I shaved this morning. I imagine that made a difference."

She smiled fully then, and it warmed him as much as the hot tin threatening to blister his hands.

"I imagine you'd like some biscuits." She stood as she spoke, and without waiting for his answer, moved to the back of the room, where she placed two golden mounds on a plate. Turning, she raised a tin. "Molasses?"

"Yes, ma'am. Thank you."

She fetched a fork and presented it to him with the plate and a quick glance. "I hope you enjoy them."

As a former man of many wo~~~
morning, he foun~
presence.

D0910360

Books by Davalynn Spencer

Love Inspired Heartsong Presents

The Rancher's Second Chance
The Cowboy Takes a Wife

DAVALYNN SPENCER's

love of writing has taken her from the national rodeo circuit and a newsroom's daily crime beat to college classrooms and inspirational publications. When not writing romance or teaching, she speaks at women's retreats and plays on her church's worship team. She and her husband have three children and four grandchildren and make their home on Colorado's Front Range with a Queensland heeler named Blue. To learn more about Davalynn visit her website at www.davalynnspencer.com.

DAVALYNN SPENCER

The Cowboy Takes a Wife

BRISTOL PUBLIC LIBRARY
1855 Greenville Rd.
Bristolville, OH 44402
(330) 889-3651

HEARTSONG
PRESENTS

If you purchased this book without a cover you should be aware
that this book is stolen property. It was reported as "unsold and
destroyed" to the publisher, and neither the author nor the
publisher has received any payment for this "stripped book."

Recycling programs
for this product may
not exist in your area.

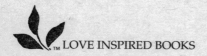 LOVE INSPIRED BOOKS

ISBN-13: 978-0-373-48697-7

THE COWBOY TAKES A WIFE

Copyright © 2014 by Davalynn Spencer

All rights reserved. Except for use in any review, the reproduction
or utilization of this work in whole or in part in any form by any
electronic, mechanical or other means, now known or hereafter
invented, including xerography, photocopying and recording, or in
any information storage or retrieval system, is forbidden without
the written permission of the editorial office, Love Inspired Books,
233 Broadway, New York, NY 10279 U.S.A.

This is a work of fiction. Names, characters, places and incidents are
either the product of the author's imagination or are used fictitiously, and
any resemblance to actual persons, living or dead, business establishments,
events or locales is entirely coincidental.

This edition published by arrangement with Love Inspired Books.

® and TM are trademarks of Love Inspired Books, used under license.
Trademarks indicated with ® are registered in the United States Patent
and Trademark Office, the Canadian Trade Marks Office and in other
countries.

www.Harlequin.com

Printed in U.S.A.

For I know the thoughts that I think toward you, saith the Lord, thoughts of peace and not of evil, to give you an expected end.
                                              —*Jeremiah* 29:11

This book is dedicated to the indomitable spirit of those who through trial have burnished their faith to shine brighter than the purest gold.

Prologue

Annie Whitaker clenched her jaw and wrapped her fingers around the arms of the front-porch rocking chair. It was better than wrapping them around her older sister's throat.

Of course Edna thought heading for the Rocky Mountains was a bad idea. *Everything* was a bad idea unless she'd thought of it first.

Perspiration gathered at the nape of Annie's neck. She uncurled her fingers and relaxed her jaw. Using her sweetest voice, she shifted to Edna's favorite topic. "Do you have your eye on any particular fella who's been calling lately?"

Edna batted a silk fan through the heavy air and lowered her gaze. The porch swing creaked as she toed it back and forth. "Maybe," she said.

Annie rolled her eyes, grateful that Edna couldn't see out the side of her head like a mule. She rubbed her cheek to hide her smile at the joke.

Annie guessed Jonathan Mitchell topped Edna's list. He

was financially successful, well-bred and handsome in a soft sort of way. And she fully expected Daddy to turn the mercantile over to Mr. Mitchell when he left next month.

When *they* left.

Annie planned to be on that stagecoach with her father come he— She stopped at the forbidden word and glanced at her sister, who always managed to read Annie's improper thoughts.

But why shouldn't she say that word? It was in the Bible. And it certainly applied to Omaha at the moment, which was heavy and hot as an unbroken fever.

Heat waves rolled over their aunt Harriet's vast lawns and rippled the distant trees into a surreal horizon. Annie unfastened the top button on her thin blouse. She detested summer—particularly July—almost as much as she disliked Edna's propensity for being coy.

"Annabelle May." Edna glared. "Don't be indecent."

"Don't be absurd." Annie released the second button out of spite. "It's unbearably hot, and there's no one to see besides you and Aunt Harriet. And she's half-blind." So much for her "sweet" voice.

"Well, I never." Edna's eyelashes whipped up the humidity even more than her fan.

Annie pushed out of the rocker and leaned over the porch railing. Even the copper daylilies bordering the Victorian home struggled to hold their heads up in the afternoon heat.

Edna's brow glistened with perspiration. "A little warmth does not give a lady license for indecency."

Tired of the heat as well as Edna's attitude, Annie stomped her foot and spun toward her sister.

"Daddy wants to go to Cañon City, and I'm going with him. You can stay here in Omaha with all your beaus and Aunt Harriet if you like, but I'm not letting our father go alone." Annie reset a loose pin in her unruly hair, then fisted her hands on her hips. "It will be an adventure. 'Pikes Peak or Bust,' they say. All those gold seekers need to get their supplies from someone. Why not Whitaker's Mercantile?"

"Humph." Edna expertly flicked her wrist, folding the hand-painted silk fan for emphasis. "That's all you think about—adventure. You and Father both." She palmed damp ringlets off her pale forehead, then reopened the fan for a fresh attack. "I can't believe he's willing to pull up and take off for those ragged mountains at his age. He should stay here and increase his holdings. The mercantile is doing quite well. Why start over someplace else and risk losing everything?" Edna fluttered furiously and aimed a guilt-inducing glare at Annie. "Including his life and yours."

Annie folded her arms. Edna's threat echoed their aunt's petulant scolding. Aunt Harriet was bound by tradition and the social constraints of widowhood, and she dripped resentment over her brother's freedom to do as he pleased.

Well, that was Aunt Harriet's choice, not Annie's. Annie preferred to experience all she could, even if it meant risking her life in the Rocky Mountains. Zebulon Pike, John C. Frémont and others had conquered those peaks. Why not Daniel Whitaker and his younger daughter?

"Cañon City isn't even established. It's an upstart supply town, Annie, on Kansas Territory's farthest edge."

Annie rested against the railing and focused on the window's beveled edge behind the swing. "I know what and where it is."

"What it *is* is uncivilized." Edna slowed her silken assault, tempered her tone. "You know what that means. They have no law yet, and probably even less order with all those gold-hungry miners and speculators and wild, drunken cowboys."

"And bank clerks and preachers and storekeepers."

Annie pressed her open neckline flat against her collar-bone. "Be reasonable."

An unreasonable request when it came to her sister.

Predictably, Edna stiffened and assumed a superior posture. "And Indians. You *know* wild savages live there, as well as all along the way. Don't forget what the Utes did at Fort Pueblo just six years ago."

Annie gritted her teeth, barring hateful words that fought for release. She and her sister had waged this verbal war about the West more times than she cared to count. She refused to chew that piece of meat again.

A rare breeze suddenly swept the wide front porch, and Annie imagined mountain air whispering along high canyons. She braced her hands against the railing, closed her eyes and recalled what she'd read about the Arkansas River falling from the Rockies, cold and full-bellied with snow-melt. A marvelously deep gorge squeezed the river into raging white water and shot it onto the high plains through a wedge-shaped valley. And guarding the mountain gateway, that brand-new town—Cañon City.

Oh, to be part of something new and unpredictable. To see that canyon, and hear the water's roar…

Edna's lofty *tsk* interrupted the daydream. "I know the stories, too." Annie's eyes flew open to see her sister's shaking head and mirthless lips. Edna read her mind as easily as a dime novel.

"Do you know that at last count Cañon City had only seven hundred and twenty residents?" Edna said.

Annie raised her chin. "Daddy and I have discussed it."

The fan snapped shut. "Do you know that out of that number *six hundred* are men?" Edna shuddered.

"They're men, Edna. Not animals."

"Don't be so sure, dear sister. With numbers like that,

I dare say those *men* are hard-pressed to maintain their humanity."

"This is 1860, not the Dark Ages." Annie stepped away from the railing, tempted to undo a third button just to see how fast Edna could flail her fan. "We are going, and we are leaving in three weeks with or without your approval—or Aunt Harriet's."

Annie marched into the house and down the hall to the kitchen, where she retrieved the lemonade pitcher from the icebox. No doubt she'd not have such a modern luxury in Cañon City. She poured a glass, let it chill with the cold drink and then held it against her forehead and neck.

The shocking relief conjured images of clear mountain snowmelt. Goose bumps rippled down her spine. The Arkansas must be delightfully cold, nothing like the Big Muddy slogging along dark and murky on its unhurried journey to the Mississippi.

At nearly a mile high, Cañon City was close to Denver City's famous claim. That in itself had to present a cooler climate. Much more pleasant, even in the summer. She figured Edna didn't know *that*.

Guilt knifed between her thoughts, and she regretted her snippy attitude. But Edna infuriated her so. How had they both come from the same parents?

Annie felt a familiar ache. That was one thing Edna did know that Annie did not—their mother's comforting arms.

She doused the pain with a sweetly sour gulp of lemonade that quite reflected the two Whitaker sisters. Annie fingered the corners of her mouth, certain that she was not the "sweet" one. She and Edna were no more alike than the dresses they wore.

Edna was polished satin. Annie, plain calico.

Was that the real reason behind her determination to go west with Daddy?

She slumped into a kitchen chair and traced the delicate needlework on the tablecloth. Several eligible young men called on the fair-haired Edna. But no one called for the wild-maned Annie.

She pushed a loose strand from her forehead as tears stung her eyes. Swallowing the dregs of jealousy, she whispered, "Forgive me, Lord. Help me love my sister. Even if I don't like her very much sometimes."

The screen door slammed against its frame, and Edna's full skirts rustled toward the kitchen.

Annie rushed to the icebox and filled a second glass with lemonade for her sister.

It was the least she could do.

Chapter 1

The late October sun bled pink and gold, impaled on an uneven ridgeline. Caleb Hutton stopped at the lip of a bowl-like depression, leaned on his saddle horn and studied the jagged silhouette. He could just make out a shadowy monolith jutting from the mountain and at its base a narrow green vein that pulsed across the valley floor. To the right a dozen buildings stood below a craggy granite spine. The faint sounds of hammers and people and livestock drifted across the valley.

Cañon City.

The fledgling town huddled north of the tree-lined Arkansas River, where canvas tents, lean-tos and campfires sprouted. Approaching from due east, Caleb crossed the valley and rode into town past a livery, corral and framed-in shops. A white clapboard building stood across from the livery—a schoolhouse or a church.

He stopped at the largest structure, the Fremont Hotel,

dismounted and looped both horses' reins around the hitching rail. Rooster tongued his bit and Sally heaved a sigh. Caleb patted the gelding's neck, slapped dust from his hat and stepped through the hotel door in need of a room and a bath.

He found neither.

Rumors had been right. The burgeoning mine-supply town was full to bursting. Every chair in the crowded parlor held a man, and laughter and cigar smoke drifted from the open doorway to the adjoining saloon. Caleb's empty stomach roiled, and he returned to his horses.

Besides the substantial brick-faced hotel, the saloon and a few other establishments, buildings in varying degrees of completion lined the short, broad street. Fading daylight drew carpenters and masons from their work and into their wagons, but others lingered along the boardwalk. Mostly miners holed up for the winter, Caleb supposed, from the looks of their grimy dungarees and whiskers.

At least he'd beat the snow.

Rooster's head drooped over the rail, eyes closed. Caleb rubbed beneath the red forelock.

"Tired as I am, are you, boy?" After gathering the reins, he mounted the gelding, pulled Sally along behind them and turned back the way he had come. The river should be running low and smooth with summer long past, and the cottonwood grove he'd seen on his approach would be hotel enough.

He'd keep the horses with him rather than board them at the livery and sleep somewhere else alone. After three months under the stars with the animals' heavy presence nearby, he doubted he could sleep without them anyway.

Come dark he'd brave the cold water for a bath.

Near the street's end, a woman swept the boards in front of a narrow storefront. Above her hung a painted wooden sign: Whitaker's Mercantile. As he rode nearer, she stooped to reclaim something, and a hunk of chestnut hair fell over her shoulder. She leaned her broom against the building and twisted her locks into a knot. He didn't realize he was staring until her eyes flashed his way, challenging his steady observation.

As he came even with the store, he touched the brim of his hat. "Evening, ma'am."

She dropped her hands as if caught stealing but held his gaze, nodding briefly before she turned away.

Caleb swallowed a knot in his throat. He reined Rooster toward the river, down the gentle slope to the cottonwood grove, and set his mind on making camp. No point digging up what he'd spent the past three months riding away from.

The horses drank their fill, and he hobbled and tethered them close by. Didn't need some hard case sneaking off with them while he slept.

The breeze danced downstream and shivered through the trees. Caleb's campfire was not the only glow along the river and he was grateful for its warmth. As he cut open his last can of beans, he counted a half dozen flickering lights scattered up and down the banks.

Beneath his saddle lay his father's old friend, a Colt revolver. Good for snakes, his pa had always said. On the backside of Kansas Territory—as anywhere—some of those snakes had two legs and would likely kill to get what they wanted. He would not fall victim.

He sank onto his bedroll, eased back against his saddle and waited for the stars to show—again. He could nearly chart them from watching them wink into view each night, as constant and familiar as his horses.

Restfulness settled over him for the first time since he'd left Saint Joseph. The muscles in his neck and legs relaxed, and tension seeped from his spine as the river chattered a few feet away like a secret companion.

Three months riding alone had given him plenty of time to think about his life, where he'd been and where he was going. One more day and he'd be at the Lazy R, where cattle outnumbered people fifty to one.

Suited him just fine.

He pulled off his hat and linked his fingers behind his head.

He knew his way around horses better than most, thanks to his pa, rest his soul. Cows weren't that much different.

At least they wouldn't be sitting in pews waiting for him to say something inspiring.

He snorted at the image, but guilt twisted his gut. He'd tried his hand at people and failed. God must have made a mistake.

Or Caleb had misheard.

A twig snapped, and he slid a hand beneath his saddle. The hammer's click cut through the silence and drew a quick confession.

"Don't shoot, mister—don't shoot."

Caleb aimed for the voice, though the tremor in it revealed the owner's young age.

"Show yourself," he ordered.

Another snap and a boy stepped from between the horses, arms raised stick straight as if he were being hung by his thumbs.

"I ain't stealin' nothin', mister—I swear."

Caleb sat up. "Right there's two things you shouldn't be doing."

Firelight licked the boy's skinny neck, and his Adam's apple bobbed. "Yessir. What's that, sir?"

Caleb eased the hammer back and lowered his gun. "Stealing and swearing. Both will get you into trouble."

He waved the boy over and kept the revolver in his lap. "How old are you, and what're you doing out here by yourself at night? Don't you know you could be shot?"

"Twelve, huntin' a bush and yes, sir."

Caleb held back a chuckle at the nervous answer. "You can put your hands down now."

The youngster dropped his arms fast. The gesture reminded Caleb of the woman at the mercantile.

"What's your name?"

"My Christian name is Benjamin, sir, but my folks call me Springer."

"Well, Springer, where *are* your folks?"

The boy pointed upstream. "See that light there in the trees? That there's our camp."

"Aren't you a little far from home for this time of night?"

"Yessir, but like I said, I was huntin' a bush."

A woman's voice called through the dark, quietly at first, then with greater urgency.

"You'd better answer," Caleb said.

"Comin', Ma."

The boy's voice cracked, and Caleb dropped his head and smiled. He poked the fire with a broken branch, and sparks licked the sky. "So, Springer, before you head back, I have two questions for you. First, tell me why they call you Springer."

The boy grinned and stuck his thumbs in his suspenders. "That's 'cause I can jump higher 'n anybody."

Life should be so simple.

"Okay. Second, why were you sneaking up on my horses?"

Springer hung his head, and his hands dropped to his sides. "I just wanted to pet 'em. We had to get rid of our horses, and I miss 'em somethin' fierce."

"Benjamin Springer Smith—I'm gonna tan your hide if you don't get your tail over here right now."

Caleb laughed out loud. "Okay, Benjamin Springer Smith, you better get going or you won't have a hide left to tan the next time."

"Yessir. Thank you, sir."

The boy crashed through the cottonwoods like a razor-back on the run. A high-pitched yelp signaled that his arrival home had not happened as quickly as his ma would have liked.

Caleb chuckled and stashed the revolver. He poked the fire again. Embers scattered like Missouri fireflies, and the wood snapped and cracked in surrender to the flames.

The sound punctured his chest, reopening a wound. He shoved the heel of his hand against his breastbone, winded by the unexpected pain.

He'd surrendered once to a searing flame. Twice, really. Answered a call that proved fruitless and offered his soul to a woman who proved faithless. Both failings twisted into a noose, and he wanted nothing but to rid himself of it.

Inexperience had cost him his life's endeavors—his small pastorate and the heart of the woman he loved. Too young to earn many converts, he thought he'd at least turned Miss Mollie Sullivan's heart.

He'd turned her all right. All the way into the arms of the wealthiest man in his congregation. Who also happened to sit on the elders' board.

He grunted and stabbed at the fire again, refusing to let it burn out. He dug for the brightest ember and held the stick against it until the wood flamed into a torch.

A similar torch had gutted him, left him ruined for both the ministry and matrimony. He refused to stand in the pulpit avoiding their eyes while he preached God's love and forgiveness. Nor could he call a meeting of the board and explain his sudden departure.

He'd simply traded his frock coat and collar for a duster and broad brim and tacked a note to the chapel door.

Not exactly Luther's *Ninety-Five Theses*.

A sneer lifted his lip.

He had wanted to smash the man's smooth-skinned face. But then he'd be no better than the thieving scoundrel himself. And what would that tell his parishioners? Turn the first cheek so he could punch the second?

He shoved the charred branch into the dirt, stretched out on his bedroll and folded his arms across his chest. For three months he'd argued with himself about returning to Saint Joe and owning up. But he'd already said his piece in the note on the door—told those gentlefolk they needed a more experienced preacher and left them the name of his seminary professor.

And if he went back and knocked out one of his congregants with anything other than preacherly conviction, he'd have to apologize all over again.

Better leave well enough alone.

He rubbed his chin, scratched at the stubble.

Tomorrow he'd start forgetting. Forget Mollie, the ministry and everything familiar, including the three people he'd met since riding into Cañon City—an apologetic hotel clerk who didn't have a room for him, a beautiful woman with a broom and a youngster camping by the river with his family. Two of the three he wouldn't mind seeing again, but that likely wouldn't happen.

Setting his boots aside, he slipped into the shallow water, submerging himself with a harsh gasp as the current wrapped around him. Cold but cleaner, he quickly dried off, dressed, stirred the fire and crawled into his bedroll.

The familiar mix of wood smoke, leather and dried horse

sweat swirled above him, and he stared at the only thing there was to see. A starry band swept across the sky, sparkling a thousand times brighter than it did in Saint Joseph. A glittering contrast to the black vault.

Not unlike the shimmer he'd seen in the broom lady's lovely eyes.

Tomorrow. He'd forget all of them tomorrow and start his new life.

Annie heard the "plop" before the smell penetrated the rough wall. Her nose wrinkled, and she buried her face in her pillow.

Never in all her seventeen years had she dreamed she'd wake up in a barn.

A horse whinnied and pawed, impatient for breakfast. Annie's stomach returned the complaint, but the stench of the fresh deposit warred with her hunger pangs. She pulled the quilt over her head and burrowed into the blankets on her straw-filled pallet.

The Overland Stage had safely carried Annie and her father across the wide prairie last month, and they'd shared some primitive accommodations along the way. But the Planter's House in Denver City and their weeklong stay there had led her to believe that maybe the rugged Rockies weren't so rugged after all.

Ha. That was Denver; this was not.

What would her sister say if she could see Annie curled up in the Cañon City Livery? A vision of Edna's tightly seamed lips and disapproving fan roused Annie's ire, and the imagined words shot heat through her veins.

I told you so.

Annie tossed the quilts back and reached for the clothing she'd draped over the foot of her pallet. After pulling her arms inside her cotton gown, she traded out the stockings and drawers she'd slept in but kept her chemise. She tugged on a flannel petticoat, topped it with two skirts, then exchanged her gown for a long-sleeved shirt and buttoned on her high-top shoes. She loosened the long braid that hung down her back and, with dexterity born of practice, brushed through the thick strands and deftly twisted them into a knot and pinned them in place.

Not that she counted on it to stay. By noon it would be hugging the base of her neck.

She smoothed her quilt top, tucked in the edges all around and prayed that no mice had worried their way into her bed looking for warmth.

A shiver scurried along her spine.

What were their chances of surviving the winter in this place? How would she and her father not freeze to death?

Needing relief, she had no time for fearful thoughts. She pulled her heavy cloak about her shoulders for a trip to the necessary.

Since she was always up before her father, Annie quietly stepped around the curtain they'd hung to separate their pallets. She stopped short. He sat at the pallet's edge, suspenders drooping off his hunched shoulders, his head in his hands.

"Daddy?" she whispered. "Are you all right?"

He raised his head, and she saw worry in his moist eyes. "*We* are not all right, Annie." He spread his hands, palms up. "Look where we are. We sleep in a *barn*. I've brought my beautiful young daughter all the way to the Rocky Mountains to live in a barn."

His head sank to his hands again.

His words burned into the doubts she'd so carefully hidden in the back of her heart. Some very hostile, unladylike thoughts of their new landlord—one Jedediah Cooper—

sparked her resolve. "Oh, Daddy, we're going to be fine." She knelt beside him and clasped his arm.

He pulled a white handkerchief from his back pocket and wiped his eyes. "We should have stayed in Omaha. My sister and yours were right."

Annie's hackles rose at the idea of Edna being right— *again.* "No, they were not. They simply don't have the adventurous streak that you and I have." She forced her lips into a smile and smoothed his uncombed hair off his forehead. "We'll talk to Mr. Cooper again about giving us the back room in the store. It's whiskey he's got in there, and he can move it to his saloon. I'll even help."

Her father's eyes latched on to hers, and his bushy brows lurched together. "You will not. You don't go near that place of his." He stuffed the handkerchief into his pocket and shook his head. "If we sold the mare, we'd have money against a loan and could build a small cabin of our own. And we'd save on her feed, too. She eats as much as the other three horses combined."

Annie stood and brushed off her skirt. It wasn't completely true—her beloved mare, Nell, didn't eat quite that much. Maybe just as much as two of their other horses, but that wasn't the point.

She buttoned her heart against her father's remark and her cloak against the cold. "I'm going out back and then to the mercantile. You banked the fire last night, so it won't take me long to get the place warmed up." She bent to kiss his snowy head. "That potbellied stove is a blessing. I'll have coffee going in no time."

Her father slapped his hands on his knees and threw back his shoulders. "You've got spunk, Annie girl. Just like your mama."

His words picked at an old scab, the one that always

opened anew when he mentioned the mother she had never known.

"I'll feed Nell, too, Daddy."

He huffed, wagged his head and grunted as he pushed to his feet.

Annie opened the stall door and gathered her skirts against her as she pulled it closed. The mare whinnied and hung her massive head over the railing across the alleyway.

"Hungry again, are you, Nell?" Annie scooped an armload of loose hay and tossed it over the gate. She brushed off her skirt again and picked stubborn pieces from her cloak.

"Take it slow, girl." Reaching over the gate, she stroked the thick golden neck and lowered her voice to a whisper. "Daddy's going to sell you like the others if you don't quit eating so much."

Nell's ears flicked forward and back as if taking due note.

They'd needed all four animals to pull their heavy supplies south to Cañon City because Daddy refused to drive mules or pay someone else to do it. But after renting and stocking the mercantile, he'd sold off the other three horses, their harness and the freight wagon. Everything excess had to go, he'd said. She'd fought dearly to keep the big yellow mare.

She checked over her shoulder for unlikely onlookers, then rubbed her backside, remembering how it ached during the jolting ride south after purchasing supplies in Denver City. The trip had been much worse than the dust-choked Overland Stage ride from Leavenworth but mercifully shorter.

Annie hurried to the shanty behind the livery, then to the boardwalk, where few people appeared so early. At the mercantile door, she slid the key in the lock and entered to the brass bell's cheerful welcome. The scent of coffee beans, tobacco and oiled leather soothed her nerves, and she drew in a slow, deep breath. Her heart swelled with pride at their modest store, full of everything a person could want—a person with a soul brave enough to head west, that is.

Fine flour and sugar, pearly oats and smooth dried beans, barrels of sour pickles and pale crackers. Bright dress cloth and drab canvas, blue-speckled dishware and cast-iron skillets. Black leather boots and shoes and a few saddles. Strong soaps, wooden toys, a precious sampling of books and notions like needles and threads and buttons and pins—better than a drummer's wagon.

Pulling off her cloak, she surveyed the cramped, full-to-the-brim space. She was useful here, working beside her father, as if what she did mattered. They met people's needs, and that was important. Much more important than sitting on Aunt Harriet's front porch waiting for one of Edna's many beaus to give her a second glance.

To pick up Annie as second best.

Disappointment clawed at her as she thought of her sister's beauty. Annie's rippling hair never stayed put like Edna's flaxen tresses, and her thin chest only half filled Edna's ruffled bodices. Daddy had called her "beautiful" this morning, but she knew she would never be as fetching as her sister.

Her chin jerked up. So be it. It was better this way, better that she didn't turn the head of every man who saw her. Her father needed help, and she refused to sit by and wait for some man to come along and make her life better when she could do that herself.

She marched to the stove that anchored the long, narrow room, bunched her skirt to protect her hand and opened the door. With a poker she scraped at the ash pile and uncovered a glowing red eye. Perfect. She added a few chunks from the nearby coal bucket and adjusted the damper.

Lord, You promised You'd meet our needs. She rubbed her hands together and held them open above the squat stove, careful not to let her skirts touch its iron belly. *And You know Daddy and I need a warmer place to stay until we can afford to build a house.*

Of course, some folks had it worse. How many were camped by the river in canvas tents, cooking over open fires?

Frustrated that she couldn't build a house with her own two hands, Annie squirmed inwardly at the doubt behind her pleading prayer.

She left the warm spot to grind fresh coffee, filled a blue enamel pot with water and set it on the stove. Satisfied with the fire, she closed the damper and arranged several chairs around a braided rug before the stove.

She and Daddy could get warm and be out of the crisp fall air. The acknowledgment settled like a warm quilt around her soul, reminding her that small blessings were still blessings.

"Thank You, Lord," she whispered, chastened.

Since her father had agreed to handle the mail for Cañon City, at least a couple hundred people trailed through the mercantile each week. Not everyone had family to write to them, and a few, she'd learned, preferred not to have folks know where they were.

In the few weeks they'd been there, her father's store had become a gathering place for several of the town's more respectable residents, as well as a few who were not—like Jedediah Cooper, their landlord, who owned nearly two blocks and acted like he owned his renters, too.

She shuddered at the memory of his whiskey-colored gaze.

With everything in order, Annie hung her wrap on the back wall that separated the mercantile from the small storeroom. She pulled an apron over her head, dislodging her hair in the process, and peeked around the doorless frame.

Anger stirred in her chest. That ol' miser Cooper should have rented them the whole building. What was eight more feet, give or take?

She tied the apron strings and quickly repinned her rebellious strands. Combs. She'd order more combs and hairpins the next chance she got. Other women must have the same problem, and combs might sell along with the gloves and hats they kept on hand.

The bell chimed.

"Smells good in here, Annie."

Relief rushed in with the return of her father's usual cheerfulness. She offered another prayer of thanks and set about greasing a cast-iron skillet. "Coffee's almost ready. Come have a seat and I'll make some pan biscuits."

He pegged his coat and donned an apron. "If the freighters stop in today, I'll mention the mare again. Then you could have a cabin with a real cookstove. Maybe an iron bed, too."

Annie swallowed at the thought of saying farewell to Nell as she floured the sideboard and rolled out the dough.

The bell rang again, and Duke Deacon and his son, Joseph, stomped in. Of course the day's first customers had to be the freighters. Who else was out this early?

By the time she had the biscuits on the stove, the men had taken chairs and coffee. Annie set to making a fresh pot, praying the freighters wouldn't want her Nell.

"Gonna be a long, hard winter, Whitaker," the elder driver said. His blue eyes shone like lights from his weathered face, and his black hair lay slick and flat against his skull. "If there's somethin' you'll be needin' 'fore spring, better order it now. I'll be freightin' 'tween storms, so won't be near as regular as it is now. Fact, this is my last trip to Denver City for a spell. When I get back, I'll be stayin' put for a couple weeks."

Her father leaned against a cracker barrel, nursing his own tin cup. "Tell me how you figure on a hard winter."

"Skunk cabbage," Joseph piped up. He was a shorter, smoother version of his coal-haired father. "Higher 'n it's been in a long time. Ain't that so, Pa."

Duke nodded and sipped. "That's right. Surprised to see it, too. Don't usually get that much snow down here 'long the Arkansas. Not like falls up on the Platte."

Annie caught her father's laughing eyes above his coffee cup. He didn't put stock in such folklore about cabbage and snowfall and hard winters, and he was more inclined to refer to the almanac he kept under the front counter. But he was good with his customers and would never say such a thing out loud.

The Deacons left with a dozen biscuits in their bellies and an order for ladies' combs and hairpins. All the cabbage talk must have driven Nell from her father's mind, and Annie heaved a sigh of relief when the freighters climbed onto their wagon without having bought her beautiful mare.

Strange, the things she'd thanked the Lord for lately.

Perspiring in the cramped store now that the stove was hot, Annie rolled up her sleeves and wiped her neck with her apron hem. No time to cool herself with a brief walk outdoors. More customers were sure to come.

She plopped a fresh batch of dough onto the floured sideboard, sending up a dusty cloud. Rolled and cut and amply greased, a second batch browned on the potbelly within minutes.

"Believe I'll buy this tin o' molasses to go with those fine biscuits you've got there." Her father stood behind the front counter, dusting the tin top with his shirtsleeve. Then he penciled the item on a notepad where he listed his personal purchases.

Annie sighed. They might freeze to death in the livery but at least they'd not starve their first winter.

Hefting the black skillet with a towel, she carried it to the sideboard, where she split two biscuits each onto two tin plates and drizzled dark molasses over both servings. After adding a fork to each plate, she joined her father already seated and waiting.

Settled and warm with food on her lap and her dear father close by, Annie's heart overflowed with gratitude as he prayed.

"Thank You, Lord, for feeding us and keeping us safe. And open Cooper's heart, Lord. Before it snows, if possible. Amen."

Refusing to let their stingy landlord's image lay claim to her thoughts, Annie forked off a bite and savored the sweet molasses-covered mouthful. She dabbed at her mouth with her apron and eyed her father, who heartily attacked his breakfast.

"You don't believe that nonsense about skunk cabbage do you, Daddy?"

He cut into the second biscuit and sopped it in the pooling molasses. "Nope." Closing his eyes, he chewed slowly and shook his head. "Delicious, Annie. Absolutely the best biscuits this side of the Rocky Mountains."

Annie swallowed another bite. "You can't say that anymore."

"And why not?"

"Because now we are *in* the Rocky Mountains, Daddy," she said, giving him the very best smile she could muster.

Chapter 2

Mollie Sullivan twittered at Caleb's sermon, and heat flooded his face. She chirped again and ducked her pretty blond head as a red-winged blackbird took flight from her Sunday bonnet.

Caleb's eyes flew open. Pink sky hung above him and birdsong filled the air. He turned his head toward the horses. Still tethered. They stomped their back feet, lipped leaves from the cottonwoods and swished their tails. Rooster looked his way and swiveled an ear.

Caleb sat up, threw back his blanket and canvas and pulled on his boots. Someone was frying bacon. Probably Springer Smith's ma, considering the direction from which the savory smell came.

He reached into his saddlebag for the last jerky strip and a biscuit he'd been saving, and laid them on his bedroll. Then he found his razor and soap, turned toward the east and stopped at the spectacle.

Low clouds tumbled on the fiery horizon, black and backlit with red and gold, splayed out like the hand of God. Unbidden came the phrase, *Your mercies are new every morning.*

Would he never stop hearing them—words he'd known as a child, handled as a man, turned his back on as a failure?

One more day.

He walked to the water's edge and squatted near an eddy. The first cold dash brought Mollie to mind again. Her image had appeared first thing every morning since leaving Saint Joseph, and he dreamed of her almost every night. But this time her features weren't as clear, and, strangely, the broom lady overlaid his fickle sweetheart's memory.

He huffed. He'd seen plenty of women in towns he'd ridden through, but none had outshone Mollie in his mind's eye when he laid down to sleep or rose in the morning—until now.

He doused the vision with another cold splash, smoothed his hand over his cheeks and checked his fingers for blood. He was getting better at shaving without a mirror. He shook out his razor, folded the wrapper around the shrinking soap bar and returned them both to the saddlebag.

His fingers brushed worn leather, and the familiar contact sent fire up his arm. He pulled out his Bible, weighed it in his hand, then shoved it back. Old habits were harder to break than an uncut yearling. But he didn't need to open those pages. The words rolled through his mind like living coals.

Two bites finished the hard tack and another the dried beef. He saddled Rooster, tied his bedroll across Sally and led the horses out of the trees. Laughter drew his gaze upstream where Springer splashed in the shallows with a small girl. A bit cold to be getting wet so early. Probably fetching water for their mother.

Cottonwood leaves fluttered like paper coins, and the treetops flashed gold as the sun found them. A warning hung in the autumn chill.

Caleb rode toward town and turned onto the main street. Two freighters climbed to their wagon box, and the larger of the men gathered the reins and called to the mules. The wagon creaked in complaint as it rolled away from the mercantile.

Had they slept by the river or under their wagon at the livery yard? Or did they have homes, loving wives and warm stoves?

Envy jabbed a finger in his gut. *Wrath killeth the foolish man, and envy slayeth the silly one.*

He shook his head to silence the voice and considered the number of fires at the river, the clusters of tents and canvas lean-tos. Stark witness to the town's greatest need.

Smoke curled a welcome from the stovepipe atop the mercantile. Good a place as any to get directions to the Lazy R. He stopped, flipped his horses' reins around the hitching rail and stepped inside.

The aroma of hot biscuits and fresh coffee nearly bowled him over. The broom lady and an older man sat close to a potbellied stove, plates balanced on their laps. Each looked up at Caleb's entrance, and the man nodded and waved him back.

"Coffee's ready. Annie just made a fresh pot."

Annie.

She watched him without expression. Her upswept hair was a chestnut-colored crown above deep, clear eyes.

Caleb removed his hat and kicked one boot against the other to knock the dust from his feet. "Thank you, sir. Coffee sounds good right about now."

The woman continued to watch as he covered the short distance and took the empty chair across from the stove.

"Mornin', ma'am," he said.

Her face came alive with recognition, and a slight smile tilted her mouth. "Now I remember. You rode by last evening, didn't you?"

"Yes, ma'am." He nodded a thank-you to the man, who handed him a cup.

"I didn't recognize you at first." She quickly scanned his attire and glanced away.

Caleb rubbed his jawline. "I shaved this morning, ma'am. I imagine that made a difference."

She smiled fully then, and it warmed him as much as the hot tin threatening to blister his hands.

"I imagine you'd like some biscuits."

She stood as she spoke and, without waiting for his answer, moved to the back of the room, where she placed two golden mounds on a plate. Turning, she raised a tin. "Molasses?"

"Yes, ma'am. Thank you."

She fetched a fork and presented it to him with the plate and a friendly glance. "I hope you enjoy them."

As a former man of many words come Sunday mornings, he found it strange to be nearly mute in her presence. "Thank you, ma'am." *Clever.*

"Name's Daniel Whitaker," the older man said, extending his hand. "Annie here is my daughter."

Caleb switched the fork to his left hand and returned the greeting. "Caleb Hutton, sir. Nice to meet you." He looked at Annie. "And you, ma'am."

Mahogany eyes flashed his way, then hid beneath dark lashes.

"Where might you be headed so late in the year, Mr. Hutton?" Whitaker sopped a biscuit and filled his mouth.

Caleb quickly swallowed a warm, sweet mouthful. "The

Lazy R. In fact, that's why I stopped in, to see if you could tell me how to get there."

"You thinking about signing on?"

"Yes, sir. I hear they're looking for hands."

Whitaker gave Caleb a smooth once-over but kept his appraisal to himself.

Annie leaned in with the coffeepot and refilled the cup he'd set at his feet. Her hair smelled like a summer day, a gentle contrast to the faint coal taste in the room.

"The Lazy R is upstream about eight miles west, but you can't follow the river," Whitaker said. "Once you get to the hot springs at the end of town, take the trail around to the right and on up a long pull. The Lazy R starts at the top. If you keep going, you'll end up in High Park and, above that, the gold fields, but that would take a day or so."

Clawing the earth for yellow ore didn't appeal to Caleb, though he knew the lure of easy money had drawn men by the thousands to these mountains. The only gold he'd ever had his eye on fell in ringlets around Mollie Sullivan's face. And he'd gone bust with her as quick as any miner in a cleaned-out claim.

"I'll find it," he said.

Eager to be on his way, he daubed the last of the molasses with a piece of biscuit and stood to take his cup and plate to the back.

Annie reached for his plate. "I'll take those, Mr. Hutton."

"Thank you again." He swallowed hard, looking for the right words. "I imagine you're as good with those dishes as you are with the broom."

A dark look sliced him in half. Her chin jutted higher, and she whirled around and strode to the cupboard at the back.

Feeling the fool, he glanced at the store owner, who wore a peculiar grin.

Caleb cleared his throat. "I meant—"

"No mind, son. We know what you meant." Whitaker pushed out of his chair and walked behind the counter, where he wrote something on a piece of paper.

Caleb plunked his hat on, regretting his woeful attempt at small talk, and dug in his waistcoat for a coin.

"No charge, Mr. Hutton," Whitaker said, raising an open hand as if forestalling an argument.

At that, Annie spun again, hands fisted at her narrow waist. Fire sparked in her eyes.

Whitaker coughed and wiped a hand across his mouth, extending the other to Caleb.

"Good luck, son. I hope you find what you're looking for."

Caleb nodded and left the store with more questions than answers. Why had Whitaker made such a remark when Caleb had clearly stated his destination? And why had Annie taken such offense at a compliment, ill-put at best?

And why did he want to see more in her eyes than ire at his foolishness?

"Daddy." Annie's left foot punctuated her frustration with a sound stomp. "We'll go broke with you giving away breakfast to every saddle tramp that wanders in here."

Her father picked up a feather duster and turned to the shelves behind the counter.

"And how many saddle tramps have we had this week, Miss Annie?"

She could see his grin, even in profile. And the old childhood endearment only added to her frustration. "Quite a few, I'd say."

"And how many did I charge for their food and supplies?" He feathered the top of a liniment tin.

She knew where this was going.

"Well?" Her father glanced her way, a glint in his eye.

"All of them." Her left foot ached for another stomp, but that childish response had prompted him to call her by her childish name. She leaned to the left and imagined pushing her shoe through the worn hardwood flooring. "Except him."

"You mean Hutton."

"Hutton. Humph."

Her father tucked the feather duster beneath the counter and folded his arms across his ample middle. "Isn't that what Edna usually says?"

Humiliation flooded her cheeks. Daddy was right. But still. "Didn't you hear what he said to me? That I must be as good at washing dishes as I am at pushing a broom?"

Her father's expression softened, but his eyes twinkled like a Christmas saint. "I think he was trying to pay you a compliment. Just take it at that and nothing more."

Some compliment. The man might have said almost anything else and done no harm. He could have mentioned the coffee, or her fresh biscuits, or…or…

Men.

She tugged her apron strings loose and cinched them tighter into a knotted bow. If she had Edna's emerald eyes and yellow hair, that drifter would have found plenty to say. But she kept that indictment to herself, recalling how sad her father had looked earlier that morning, hunched over on his pallet.

The memory doused her fury, and she slipped behind the counter and planted a kiss on his cheek. "Never you mind, Daddy. We'll get enough customers to make up for that cowboy."

She hoped. Sometimes her father had more generosity in his heart than common sense in his head.

Annie returned to the back and set water on the stove for washing their dishes.

That drifter's insult would not have stung so if it had come from a common-looking man. One that didn't carry himself with bridled confidence. One without two dark pools for eyes and the breath of untamed country about him.

She scraped a soap curl into the water and added the plates, forks and cups. By the time she had the counter cleaned, steam rose from the dishpan. Was it her imagination, or did water boil quicker in Cañon City than in Omaha?

Certainly her emotions seemed to. Just the thought of Hutton's expression as he'd downed her biscuits made her pulse kick up.

How could Daddy be so generous where customers were concerned and so stingy toward Nell?

Flustered, she moved the pan to the back counter, nearly scrubbed the white specs from the blue enamelware and soaked her apron in the process.

Nell was too big to be a pet, but she was the next best thing. Annie loved the horse's warm breath on her face, the large, kind eyes and the velvety nose that sniffled her hand for dried apples.

Guilt wiggled under Annie's collar at the purloined apple rings she sneaked into her skirt pockets each evening to treat the ever-hungry mare. Daddy wasn't the only one who gave away food. But if he kept squandering their profits on cowhands like Caleb Hutton, they'd have barely enough to live on and would need to sell the mare for sure. She rubbed angry tears away with the back of her hand at the very thought.

The bell clinked, and she turned to see Martha Bobbins flutter through the door with her customary smile.

"Oh, Daniel dear. I'm so glad to see you're here this morning."

"Daniel Dear" shot a nervous glance toward Annie and tugged at his apron straps.

Annie hid her giggle over the dishpan. Martha Bobbins certainly lived up to her name. The woman bobbed in at least once every day to buttonhole Annie's father with a "dire necessity." As the only seamstress in town, she made everything from dresses to dungarees, and she depended on Whitaker's Mercantile to supply her needs. She even had a foot-treadle sewing machine. Not many people knew about it, but Annie had seen it when she'd delivered several lengths of denim to Martha's tidy cabin.

But Annie knew that the plump little widow came in mostly to see her father, and it didn't bother Annie one bit. Martha's material needs couldn't begin to outweigh her father's need of attention from a woman his own age— someone other than his monopolizing sister, Harriet. Which was the best reason Annie could think of for moving to Cañon City, a town much too uncivilized for the likes of her aunt.

Forgive me, Lord.

Yes, Martha Bobbins was more than welcome.

Annie dried her hands on her apron, adjusted the pins slipping from her heavy hair, then joined her father and Martha at the front. Already he blushed as Martha fussed over the fabric he'd spread on the counter.

This time she fingered a creamy silk.

"I think this will be perfect for the bride, Daniel." Martha snared him with a knowing glance. Annie's father flushed crimson.

"That *is* lovely, isn't it?" Annie said, rescuing him from a painful position. She stepped close to his side and patted his back. "We were right to bring it. Weren't we, Daddy?"

He cleared his throat and pulled at his mustache. "Thanks to your good judgment, Annie."

She unfolded the fabric, extending a long, smooth swath. "And whose dress are you making, Martha, if I may pry?"

Martha twittered and waved Annie's self-judgment aside. "Hannah Baker. She and the Reverend Robert Hartman are getting married after Christmas. Don't you think that is the most romantic thing you ever heard?"

Martha's smile weakened as Daniel slipped away, and Annie reached across the silk to touch her arm. "I couldn't agree more."

Disappointment edged the little woman's eyes, and she sighed heavily.

Annie leaned over the counter and whispered, "Give him time, Martha. You're making headway."

The comment colored Martha's cheeks with a youthful blush, and a giggle escaped from behind one hand. "You really think so?"

Annie patted her arm and then straightened. "So why are Hannah and Pastor Hartman waiting until after Christmas?"

"His brother—also a preacher, you know, from up in Denver with a fancy brick church *and* a steeple—said he couldn't get down to do the ceremony until after all the holiday fuss. Hopefully he won't get snowed in. You know how we always get a heavy storm before the New Year."

Annie nodded as she unfolded several more yards of the luxurious fabric, though really she *didn't* know. It was her first winter in Cañon City.

Could Reverend Hartman's brother marry her father and Martha during the same visit?

How presumptuous. She should let her father propose first. And, of course, if he did, Annie faced a solitary future. Caleb Hutton's handsome face worked into her memory with shocking clarity. Annie shuddered.

"Are you still sleeping in that drafty old barn, dear?"

Annie glanced at the small but sprightly source of local gossip. Of course Martha knew about their living arrangements. There was nothing in town that Martha did *not* know.

"For the time being," Annie said. She lowered her voice. "I'm hoping to speak to Mr. Cooper later today and convince him to rent us the *entire* store. We could turn the back into a sleeping room of sorts."

Martha *tsked* and shook her head. "What a leech he is. Pardon me, dear, but it's the gospel truth. He shouldn't ask one penny more than you already pay, the old coot. I've a mind to charge him double for the next apron he orders from me, just to show him."

Annie laughed and folded the fabric into a smooth square. Then she wrapped it in brown paper and tied it with twine.

Martha dug in her reticule for a silver coin and handed it to Annie. "I wish I had an extra room in my cabin, and I'd have you and your father stay there." She stole a quick peek toward the back and pushed an imaginary stray lock beneath her ruffled cap.

"And you're a sweetheart for even thinking of us," Annie said as she made change and wrote out a receipt. "Thank you ever so much, but don't you worry. I'm sure I can talk Mr. Cooper into being a bit more generous before the snows come."

Annie hoped that merely saying the words out loud would make them true. But she knew better than that. She was going to have to be clever when it came to Mr. Cooper. She just didn't know quite how yet.

Chapter 3

Caleb followed the river upstream to where it cut through a granite canyon and around a jutting red rock sentinel west of town. Two log cabins squatted in a cottonwood grove. He guessed the mineral springs were at hand, for the Ute Indians he'd heard of camped several hundred paces away against a sheer rock wall. Their fires sent smoke spiraling above a stony ridge.

Surely the river was a certain path to the high country grassland, but Daniel Whitaker had said the banks choked off a few miles in. Caleb didn't have daylight to waste on a hunch, so he turned back and headed north along a narrow valley. It climbed beneath a sawtooth ridge—evidence enough for how the Rockies came by their name.

The yellow ridge scraped sky on Caleb's right, and orange sandstone abutments jutted from the hillside like upraised floorboards. To his left, Fremont Peak's lesser points pushed skyward, a prehistoric beast straining against its

rocky confines. Strange country, this land that drew cattle-
men and gold seekers alike.

Ahead the trail curved deeper into the mountains toward his longed-for escape. He hoped to make the Lazy R
by early afternoon.

Rooster's head bobbed to his steady gait, and the rocking
rhythm set Caleb's thoughts to churning. Annie Whitaker's
sweet biscuits sure beat the hard tack he'd choked down
earlier that morning. Why hadn't he mentioned *that* instead
of how handy she was with a broom?

He touched his boot heels to Rooster's side. The horse
quickened his pace but not enough to outdistance thoughts
of molasses-colored eyes that warmed Caleb's insides.

A woman like that would make a man's life brighter in
this bleak country. Be it laughter or anger, light danced in
those eyes.

To distract himself, he reached forward and grabbed
a handful of Rooster's coarse mane, pulling his fingers
through it.

Annie's hair must be soft as a baby's whisper.

He jerked his hand back. He had to be loco. After his
remark that morning, Annie Whitaker wouldn't give him
another biscuit if her life depended on it, much less the
chance to touch her hair.

Caleb angled his horses west as they climbed between
scrubby peaks. Bent and twisted juniper soon gave way to
scattered pinion and cedars that stretched against a cloud-
less blue. Air as fresh and fine as he'd ever breathed filled
his lungs with promise and his heart with hope. He could
start over here. Find his footing again.

By midday the trail broke into a wide plateau dotted with
grazing cattle. Several hundred head, he figured. In the
distance, low buildings hugged the base of a steep rise—
the Lazy R ranch house and barns. Caleb touched his heels

to Rooster's side, and the gelding eased into a gentle lope. Cool water, a pile of hay and a new life lay just across the grassland.

He slowed to a trot as he approached a gated entrance bearing a leaning *R*. As he pulled up, he studied the carver's handiwork that hung high between two massive timbers, then rode beneath and took the next quarter mile at a walk. Anticipation rose in his chest. The payoff for his long trip was close at hand.

The main barn shaded two cowboys and a horse. One man stooped beneath the saddled mount's back leg, his rasp scraping through the thin air as he smoothed the hoof. A vaquero held the reins, his leggings trimmed with a line of silver conchos.

The shoer dropped the foot, and both men eyed Caleb and his horses as they stopped at the corral.

Caleb nodded. "Afternoon."

He stepped off Rooster, flipped the reins over the top rail and offered his hand. "Caleb Hutton. I hear you're looking for ranch hands."

The shoer shook Caleb's hand but cut a glance at the vaquero.

"Where'd you hear that?"

"Saint Joseph, Missouri. In the paper there. I saw an ad for the Lazy R."

The man's eyes flicked over Caleb like Daniel Whitaker's had, but this time judgment followed.

"We got all we need. You're too late."

Caleb's heart stumbled. "I'm good with horses. Doctor livestock, too."

The vaquero's shaded eyes cut away to the near hills.

The shoer spit a black stream to the side, then wiped his mouth on his sleeve.

"No more bunks, son. Sorry, we're full up." He turned

away, slid the rasp into a small wooden box and unbuck-led his leather apron.

Caleb rehearsed the miles he'd ridden. He couldn't make it back to Missouri before winter. He cleared his throat, pushed through the tightness.

"Are there other ranches around here in need of a hard worker?"

The vaquero swung onto the horse. Sunlight glinted off his long-roweled spur as he reined the horse around and headed for the nearest bunch of cows. The farrier plopped a brown bowler on his head and squinted at Caleb.

"Wrong time o' year. Winter's comin' on, and most spreads are gettin' ready to hunker down. No brandin', nothin' that calls for extra help till spring. Come back around then."

"But the ad—"

"There's a lot o' men lookin' for work, son. We filled up quick." A black spot flew from his mouth and darkened the dirt at his feet. "Try the saloon in town. Hotel might have somethin' for you with all the miners comin' down for winter. Or the sawmill."

Reality slapped Caleb, cold and hard. He'd been a fool. Gone off half-cocked on no more than a paper promise. He'd not bunk at the Lazy R tonight or anytime soon.

He wanted to rant—holler about the miles he'd ridden, the dust he'd eaten, the new start he had to find. He wanted to preach about turning away the poor and the destitute. But he was no longer a preacher. He had no right.

He stripped the reins from the fence and climbed into the saddle. "Thanks anyway."

The first sign of emotion crossed the man's face. "Sorry, son, that's just how it is. Hope you make out." Then he grabbed the toolbox and walked into the barn.

Caleb reined Rooster back the way they'd come. He

wasn't about to ask for a place to sleep for the night, or even water for his horses.

He did not beg.

At the high gate, he headed east for Cañon City and heeled Rooster into a lope. The sun pressed toward the peaks behind him, on the run from the coming night. It pulled its warmth with it and threw a brassy light on the ridge ahead, where yellow flared through a dark pine blanket.

Caleb had read about the aspen that flecked the mountains—those white-barked trees that bore gold men didn't hunt, the kind that showed itself year after year as witness to a providential hand.

He snorted. Providence. That was one thing he didn't need.

Providence had drawn him away from his father's wishes and proven livelihood. Providence had left him without a bride, a living or a place to lay his head. And Providence had led him to the hollow hope of a fresh start.

His gut knotted against the blasphemy, and he kicked Rooster into a dead run. Maybe Providence wasn't to blame.

Maybe he had done all those things to himself.

Cooper hadn't been in for his mail, and Annie fumed. When she *didn't* want to see him, he managed to slither in and curl himself around their stove, following her with his glassy eyes. But today he kept his distance.

Well, she wasn't afraid to meet him in his own territory, despite her father's warnings. She'd be in and out of that saloon like a needle through a quilt and they'd be sleeping warmer because of it.

"Daddy, can you mind the store while I run an errand?" Annie exchanged her apron for her cloak and fastened it up to her neck. She'd not give Cooper and his kind anything to look at.

She reached the door before her father answered and paused with her hand on the knob. She looked over her shoulder for his whereabouts.

"Hurry back." The front counter muffled his reply, and he stood, red-faced from bending over.

Annie's nerves pushed her out the door before he had a chance to ask her destination.

She pulled her hood against her neck and drew deep satisfaction from her heels clacking on the boardwalk. Mr. Jedediah Cooper would agree to her terms, or wish he had. How dare he force them to live in the livery stable while his whiskey cases littered the back room?

At the end of the block, she stepped into the dirt street and hurried across to the walkway that fronted the Fremont Hotel and Saloon. People around here certainly were fond of John C. Frémont. It's a wonder they hadn't named the town after the explorer.

She slowed her steps as she approached the saloon, well aware that unmarried women were the exception in this town and did not show their faces in drinking establishments unless they, well, weren't good, churchgoing women. But she had to talk to Cooper, and she didn't want to wait for him to slink down to the store for his precious whiskey. She and her father needed a better roof over their heads and they needed it now.

Her left heel involuntarily stamped the boards. Oh— she had to control that reflex or Cooper would laugh her out of his saloon.

Stretching to her full height, she raised her chin and opened one of the saloon's double doors, catching her flushed reflection in the oval glass.

Nearly empty this early in the day, the space could

easily have passed for a ballroom had it not been for the tables and the long mirrored bar against the west wall. Cooper himself stood behind it, his head bent as if ciphering his accounts. The stale scent of tobacco seeped from the red-and-gold-papered walls, and the odor cloaked her like a shroud.

Annie pulled the door closed and cleared her throat.

Cooper looked up, his frown melting into a lascivious leer as he recognized his caller.

Annie's left hand still held the doorknob. Her grip tightened.

"Come in, come in, my dear child." Cooper tugged at his brocade waistcoat and made his way from behind the bar, weaving slowly through the empty tables like a python to its prey. "What brings you to the Fremont this fine day?"

Wishing she'd worn gloves, she accepted his moist hand in a brief greeting, then quickly balled her fingers beneath her wrap.

"I want to discuss renting the entire store from you, Mr. Cooper." She held his gluttonous glare, determined to keep up a bold front in his presence.

He gestured to the nearest table and pulled out a curved-back chair. "Please, be seated, Miss Whitaker. Care for a brandy?"

Her throat tightened. "No, thank you. I simply want to discuss the store. If you recall, my father and I rent the front half and more, but there remains a small space behind the dividing wall that we could use."

For living quarters, but he didn't need to know that.

His eyes swept her length and back again, as if tearing the cloak from her, and then settled on the hand that held the doorknob as he stepped closer.

Sensing how she must appear a frightened child, she let

go but stood firmly in place. "How much more do you need for the use of all the floor space?"

Cooper shifted his appraisal to the fingers of his right hand. He curled them against his palm as if examining his nails. "I'm using that space for storage right now."

"I understand, but surely you have room for your whiskey cases here in the saloon." She reviewed her rehearsed argument. "Perhaps behind the bar or in a back room where they would be much handier, don't you think?"

She scanned the room and noted two closed doors—one near the bar that led to the hotel and one at the opposite end of the back wall. "I'm sure my father will be happy to help you relocate the crates."

Cooper's eyes matched his beloved amber liquor. No doubt they hid as much evil in their depths as the corked bottles behind Annie's makeshift kitchen.

"Well, it will inconvenience me, but I suppose we might work out an arrangement."

Her skin chilled at the insinuation in his shadowed gaze. If she and her father didn't need a warmer place to stay this winter, she'd slap that disgusting smirk right off his puffy face.

The door smacked her hard in the back. Both hands flew up as she fell against Cooper's chest. Fighting to regain her balance, she pulled from his clutches and whirled to see who had hit her with the door.

Two men quickly yanked off their hats as they realized what had happened.

"Excuse me, ma'am," one said in a rush. "I'm sorry—I didn't expect anyone to be standing so close to the door. Especially a lady. I should have been more careful." He bobbed his head like a worried goose and fled to the safety of the bar. His companion she recognized as Magistrate

Warren, who frowned at Cooper, replaced his hat and followed.

Cooper's eyes focused on Annie's right cheek, and she quickly reached for the hair knocked loose by the sudden jolt. She tipped her head and repinned the mass, furious that her hair betrayed her when she was bargaining with such a pagan.

He coughed, regained his composure and waved a hand in dismissal. "It's yours," he said. "I'll send someone round to pack up the crates. No need to concern your father."

Startled by the greedy man's sudden change of heart, she sensed the need to keep a sober face. He wasn't the type to give anything away—unlike her father. Unless they came to some financial agreement, Annie didn't trust him to abide by his generosity.

"Mr. Cooper, I insist on paying for the space."

A storm gathered in his eyes.

Realizing her blunder, she recanted. "Thank you, Mr. Cooper. We do appreciate your generosity. Would you be so kind as to take a small additional amount each month?"

Distracted, Cooper glanced at Warren and the other man waiting at the bar and tugged at his waistcoat. He fingered a gold watch, flipped its cover open for a quick reading and returned it to a shallow pocket.

"Whatever you say, Miss Whitaker. Write up an agreement and give it to my man when he comes for the crates."

He bowed a brief goodbye and left her standing at the entrance to the saloon.

Annie exited and quietly shut the door behind her. Her heart threatened to leave her there and race ahead as she strode toward the mercantile.

She'd done it.

Or had something else changed Jedediah Cooper's mind and opened his miserly grip?

No matter. She and her father would not freeze this winter, or have to traipse through the mud and snow to get to the store. *Thank You, Lord.*

The bell above the door announced her return, and she hurried to the back and hung her wrap. Her father sat near the stove, coffee in hand. She hoped he'd forgive her blatant disobedience when he learned of her success with Mr. Cooper.

"What took you out in such a hurry, Annie?"

His dear, trusting face turned her way.

Lord, forgive me for going against his wishes.

She snugged her apron around her waist, retied the string and planted a kiss on his cheek. Could they afford the extra rent? And how much should they pay? Enough to keep Cooper from thinking they were robbing him, but not so much that they couldn't get by.

No more free biscuits to passing strangers.

And no more dried apples for Nell. Or not as many.

Promising herself that someday she'd have china dishes again, she filled a tin cup with coffee.

"I've made a deal, Daddy, and I need your help." She settled into the chair next to him. "And I need you to promise you won't be angry."

His brow dipped, and a cloudy look banished the earlier calm. "What have you done now, Annie?"

She held the cup below her lips and blew across the hot liquid. "I found us a place to stay." His stare bore into her until she felt it melting away all her good intentions. "Now, Daddy, you mustn't be upset. You know we can't spend the winter in the livery. We'd freeze."

"There are no rooms at the hotel." His voice was flat. "I check on a regular basis."

"You're right." A hasty sip and she jerked her head back, her lip protesting against the hot coffee.

"Where did you go?"

She lowered the cup to her lap, straightened her back and focused on the stove. "I spoke with Mr. Cooper, and he agreed to let us rent the *entire* store. Now we can live in the back like we talked about." She peeked at her father's face. "Isn't that wonderful?"

Not one to raise his voice—unlike her—Annie's father clamped his lips together. His silence had been worse than any punishment he'd doled out when she was a child, and she hated it just as much now.

They were partners. Equal in this endeavor. He had to stop thinking of her as a woman to be protected and realize that she could help him. *Had* helped him.

She turned in her chair to face him. "Isn't that grand?"

His eyes dulled with disappointment and sadness. "You went to the saloon, didn't you?"

She huffed out a sigh. At least the truth was out.

"Yes, I did. But before you say it's not proper for me to go there, please hear me out. It was nearly deserted so early in the day, and I asked Mr. Cooper how much he wanted for the back room and told him how much handier it would be for him to have all his whiskey close at hand instead of here, and—"

Her father reached over and squeezed her arm. "Oh, my Annie. You torment me so. It's not safe for you to be so bold."

Like a child, she squirmed beneath his rebuke. But his eyes shimmered and his voice softened. "You are so like your mother."

The old ache seeped into her chest. "Please be happy for us," she whispered.

His gray eyes swept her face, and he raised one bushy brow. "How much?"

"That's the strangest thing," she said. "We were discussing it when Magistrate Warren and another man came in. Mr. Cooper abruptly said for me to name my price and give a note to the man he'd send for the whiskey crates."

No need to mention being knocked unceremoniously into the pagan's arms.

Her father rubbed his forehead. "We can give him what we pay for the livery stall. We can afford that much."

Annie's mind breezed through the figures. "We already rent the store. And you and I both know he should have included the back room to begin with. Let's give him half what we pay for the livery stall."

Her father leaned back in his chair and studied her with a calculating air.

"What?" she said.

"You are *exactly* like your mother." This time he chuckled and stood to refill his cup. "Write the ticket and I'll push all the crates closer to the back door so they'll be handy for whoever comes to get them."

Annie rushed to throw her arms around his neck, jostling his coffee. "Thank you, Daddy. Won't it be wonderful? Almost like a real house."

He cupped one of her shoulders in his big hand and set her at arm's length. "Maybe we could fit a small cookstove in that cramped space."

"I'm in no hurry." She straightened her apron and gave him a sideways look. "Besides, I think my potbellied biscuits are quite good, if I do say so."

He laughed and set his cup on the edge of the stove.

"Potbellied, are they now?" He patted his girth with both hands. "I will be, too, if I keep eating them like I did this morning."

This morning.

Annie turned away to hide her sudden blush. Others had also savored her biscuits this morning, but thoughts of one man in particular made her heart flutter like Edna's silken fan.

The dark-eyed drifter had managed to do much more than stir her anger.

Chapter 4

Caleb bypassed Main Street and pointed Rooster toward the river. If someone hadn't beaten him to it, he'd bed down where he'd spent the previous night.

Campfires flickered in the trees along the bank, and cook smoke made his empty stomach groan. Laughter and happy voices floated downstream.

He grunted, begrudging such people their homeless pleasures. Or maybe they weren't homeless. Maybe a campsite by the river was home enough if shared with family—like Springer Smith and his folks.

The Son of Man has nowhere to lay His head.

Like a red-hot coal, the phrase scorched his thoughts. He didn't miss the irony of having more in common with Christ now than he had all those months at the parsonage. The Women's Society hadn't let him miss many meals.

A moonless night shrouded the river, and he settled for an unfamiliar clearing when he saw that his spot had indeed been taken. He hobbled the horses, tied them together and looped a lead rope around his saddle horn. At least he'd *feel* it if someone tried to steal them. Or he'd be trampled to death by his startled mounts.

The open fire warmed his face and feet and offered an odd companionship, another voice to counter that of the river, making him feel not so alone. The remains of his jerky teased his stomach into true hunger, and he drank several tin cups of water from the cold river. Again glittering stars filled the sky, reminding him that not many such nights remained before storms gathered in the mighty Rocky Mountains.

Where to now? His stomach knotted at the thought of tending bar. He may not be saving souls anymore—not that he'd had even a single convert—but he couldn't bring himself to encourage men along the road to perdition.

The sawmill was a possibility. The hotel? No. If opportunity didn't show its face tomorrow, he'd return to the mercantile for supplies and ride north to Denver. He'd have a better chance of finding work in an established city.

But cities didn't appeal to him.

Shunning prayer, he rolled to his side and closed his eyes.

Maybe Cañon City had a newspaper. He wrote well enough.

As soon as he thought of town, Annie Whitaker materialized in her long white apron, and he questioned his motives for thinking of staying. He could almost smell the fresh biscuits in her skillet as he saw her in his mind's eye.

Maybe tomorrow she'd invite him to stay for breakfast.

He grunted. And maybe he'd walk on water. Stroll right across the swirling Arkansas without even getting his boots wet.

When he woke the next morning, Caleb discovered that

pride was one thing, hunger another. He hadn't eaten in twenty-four hours.

His stomach twisted with a surly growl, and he sat up and rubbed his face. A jay scolded from a nearby thicket, and the river laughed over rocks and swirled through eddies, mocking his need.

He palmed his jaw. Only one day's growth. Not enough for a razor unless it was Sunday. But it wasn't. And even if it was, that didn't matter anymore.

He pulled on his boots, stirred the fire to dead ash, then saddled Rooster and rode into town.

The Whitakers would be up and around by now, feeding that potbellied stove so they could feed stragglers like him. He imagined Annie rolling out dough and lining her cast-iron skillet with perfect biscuit rounds. And smiling at him like she had yesterday morning before he'd made a fool of himself.

He wondered if he'd ever find his way around words again. What would it take for Annie Whitaker to grace him with her good food—and her warm smile?

Few people walked the streets, and he gave more notice to the buildings and storefronts. A bank. An assay office. A printing office. He'd check there first.

Right after he ate.

He stopped at a corner and twisted in his saddle to eye the other end of town. A few small cabins huddled this side of the white clapboard building across from the livery.

He snorted. If the clapboard was a church, there sat two callings—or so he had thought—faced off one against each other.

He turned back around, heeled Rooster's side and let the gelding amble along until they came to the mercantile. The sun was a good half hour above the horizon, and smoke spun from the store's chimney. He stepped off and flipped the reins around the rail, hoping for the same greeting he'd received the previous day but doubting he'd get it.

His mouth watered, and his heart raced. He jingled the few coins he had left in his pocket, figured he had enough for hard tack and a can of beans. Some dried beef, maybe ground coffee.

He caught his reflection in the window. Discouragement stared back, cold and calloused. He swallowed and opened the door.

As he'd hoped, the smell hit him full force. Annie Whitaker stood at the back, working at a long counter. Her father sat in his chair near the stove, coffee in hand. He raised his cup in welcome.

"Come on in, son. Didn't expect to see you back so soon."

Caleb cleared his throat and removed his hat.

Annie looked up with a question that soured to a frown. He'd apologize if she gave him the chance.

He nodded at Daniel. "Don't mind if I do."

Whitaker stood, poured a second cup and handed it to Caleb as he took a chair.

"Thank you kindly." He hung his hat on his knee and smoothed his hair back, knowing he had to look a sight after two nights by the river, sleeping in his shirt.

"Thought you'd be cuttin' cows at the Lazy R by now. You change your mind?"

Caleb sucked in a breathy taste of the hot brew, trying not to burn his mouth.

"I didn't, but they did." He glanced toward Annie, who had turned her back. "Other men must have read that ad in the paper and beat me to the job."

"That right?" Whitaker said, raising his white brows.

"Said they were full up. No room in the bunkhouse, didn't need any more hands."

"Hmm." Whitaker scratched his clean-shaven cheek. "So you heading back home?"

Home. If Caleb knew where that was, he'd gladly head that way. When his pa died, the bank took their small acreage, and at the time, Caleb had the church.

Now all he had was a kind look from the storekeep.

He shook his head. "I'll try to find something here in town and stay the winter, then head for Denver come spring. If nothing turns up by tomorrow, I'll leave the day after."

"Got your sights on gold?" The older man eyed him over his tin mug.

"No, sir. I'm not of a mind to dig for shiny ore. But I'll do about anything else if it's honest work."

A clear "ha" sounded from beyond the potbellied stove, and a grin spread across Whitaker's face.

Caleb glanced from father to daughter. "The foreman suggested I check at the saloon or motel, but I'm not much on pouring whiskey, and I doubt I'd make a very good chambermaid."

This time, Caleb heard a distinct snort from the sideboard. Whitaker's stomach bounced as he stifled a laugh, and Caleb couldn't keep a twitch from his lips. Caught in the swift current of gaiety, which he had not experienced in a very long time, he leaned closer to Whitaker. "Do you need someone to help sweep the front walk?"

Any moment the skillet would fly.

Annie spun in a skirted flurry and stomped to the stove with a batch of freshly cut biscuits. She slammed it down, adjusted the damper and skewered Caleb with a glare.

"I can handle the sweeping myself, Mr. Hutton, as you so clearly pointed out on your last visit."

Caleb saw his opportunity. He stood. "About that, Miss Whitaker. Please accept my apology. It's biscuit making at which you excel. I meant no disrespect."

She balled her fingers on her hips and kept her chin in the air, but her face softened. Dashing a russet strand from her forehead, she mumbled some epithet and whirled away.

Caleb dropped into his chair, realizing it was going to take more than a compliment about biscuits to win over Annie Whitaker.

"What do you *really* do, son?" her father said with a twinkle in his eye. "What did you do back in— Where are you from?"

"Missouri. Saint Joseph." Caleb fought off the vision of the stone church he'd left behind. "I have a way with horses, sir." *But not people. And especially not women.*

"Have you inquired at the livery? Henry might put you to work." Whitaker paused, and an idea clearly crossed his ruddy features. "You could bunk there if you don't mind a stall. I happen to know there's one available—it's only a little warmer than where the horses are, but there'd be a roof over your head come winter."

Caleb nodded and eyed the biscuits browning on the stove. "I'll look into that. Thank you."

"And when you get there, look in on the big palomino and tell me why she's nearly eating me out of my profits. I'm wanting to sell her." He glanced at his daughter. "But Annie thinks she's a pet and sneaks dried apples to her every night after we close up."

Annie peeked over her shoulder, worry etching her fine brow. Fine brow? Since when did Caleb notice a woman's brow? Or think of it as *fine?*

"I'll do that, first chance I get."

Annie moved to the stove and picked up the skillet. Warm sourdough wafted through the room, and Caleb nearly had to holler to cover his stomach's impatient rumbling. Then she delivered two deep plates with biscuits floating in dark molasses.

One for her father and one for him.

"Thank you, darlin'," Whitaker said with a tender smile.

Caleb looked into eyes the same color as the sweet molasses and nodded, afraid of what would come out of his mouth if he tried to express the gratitude he felt in that moment. "Miss Whitaker."

She met his gaze without anger, false humility or the coy flutter at which Mollie Sullivan had so excelled. Strong and confident, but kind, she returned his look, as if willing to meet him on level ground.

"It's Annie," she said.

His heart curled up like a pup on the hearth. Maybe he had a chance for a fresh start after all.

Annie feared she'd drop the plate if Caleb Hutton didn't take it from her right that instant. His dark scrutiny unsettled her, as if he saw through her bravado and into her quivering heart.

As unexpected as snow in summer, his apology had all but doused her anger. What kind of man apologized to a woman he didn't know? In front of her father, no less?

A good man.

She stepped back, flushed with heat from the stove. Loose hair stuck to her forehead and neck, and she retreated to the counter where her own plate waited. Dare she join the men in her condition?

Turning her back, she stretched her apron hem between her hands and flapped it before her face. What she wouldn't give for one of Edna's painted silk fans.

She drew a deep breath, pushed her hair off her neck and with plate in hand walked calmly to the chair farthest from Caleb Hutton.

"You've outdone yourself again, Annie girl. We should have opened a café instead of the mercantile."

After adjusting the plate on her lap, she swirled a biscuit bite in molasses, embarrassed by her father's compliment in Caleb's presence. "Thank you, Daddy, but I do believe you are prejudiced."

"He's right," Caleb said between bites. "'Course then there'd be no place to get supplies."

He smiled her way, or as close as he could come to a smile with his mouth full. She dropped her gaze to her plate and wondered what Edna would say at this point. Oh, she knew what her sister would say. She'd bat her thick lashes, wave the remark away with a milk-white hand and say, *Oh, you shouldn't carry on so. They're just plain ol' sourdough biscuits.*

"Thank you, both," Annie managed without looking up.

"If word gets out about your cooking, we may have to set a table in here."

Her father's words sparked hope, but they had no room for a table. Besides, they didn't have a real cookstove yet, and she couldn't do more than biscuits, pan gravy, eggs or beans and coffee on the old iron hunk they did have.

"Maybe I'll paint a sign—Annie's Potbellied Biscuits, Five Cents." He held up a hand as if displaying the imaginary notice for all to see.

Caleb's mouth curved up on one side. "Potbellied biscuits?"

Annie felt the flush return to her neck. "It's the stove, Mr. Hutton. The potbellied stove, and I dare say I don't think I'd care to spend the day cooking over that bootwarmer."

"Caleb, ma'am." He cast an earnest look her way. "I'd be pleased if you'd call me Caleb."

Her father suddenly stood with his plate and cup and made for the front counter. "I never did sort yesterday's mail," he scolded himself. "I must be getting old and forgetful. You two go on without me. I'll just be killin' two birds with one stone over here."

Forgetful, my eye. Annie speared the last biscuit piece. She'd be having a few words with her father after Caleb Hutton left.

Thankful she hadn't sat next to him, she slid a glance his way and noticed how seriously he consumed his food. As if his life depended on it. Instantly remorseful, she realized that he might very well depend on what she served. Where else in Cañon City would he find a meal, other than the Fremont Hotel, which always had more patrons than tables and chairs?

She laid her fork in her plate. "There's more, Mr. Hut— Caleb. Would you like a couple more biscuits?"

"Thank you." He gave her a sober look and a nearly clean plate. "They really are good."

At the counter, she opened two biscuits, covered them with thick syrup and, for no reason she could name, plucked an apple from a bowlful she was saving for pie. She cored and sliced it with a paring knife and fanned it out next to the biscuits. On her way past the stove, she lifted the coffeepot.

"More coffee?" She held out the plate and watched his reaction.

His eyes found hers. "You sure you can spare this apple?"

"We have plenty. Apple trees grow around here nearly as well as skunk cabbage." She filled his tin cup and, straightening, smoothed her apron with one hand. "If you have everything you need, I'll be in the back room unpacking."

"Unpacking stores? I can help if you need."

His sincerity gave her pause, but she turned away from his scrutiny. "No. Thank you."

She set the coffeepot on the stove and fled through the doorless opening into what was now her new home. Back-

ing against the dividing wall, she fanned her apron in her
face, feeling she'd barely escaped from—what?

She surveyed their few belongings and the scant space.
They'd been so eager to leave the livery before Cooper
changed his mind that they'd hauled everything to the store
before Annie had a chance to clean the long-neglected
room. Dusty cobwebs laced the ceiling corners, and even
more dust covered the windowsill. The entire room needed
a good sweeping and washing down, but she'd not pick up
the broom with Caleb Hutton around.

Boot steps headed for the back, and she stooped near
a carpetbag, pretending to be busy. Tin dishes clinked together in the wash pan on the sideboard. A quick glance
over her shoulder revealed her father stuffing mail in letter
boxes behind the front counter. It had to be Caleb washing his plate.

She paused in her hasty riffling through the satchel's
contents and imagined him scrubbing the sticky syrup.
He must not be married, for surely a man with a wife simply assumed that a woman tended to the dishes. Even her
father hadn't helped in the kitchen, always relying on his
sister and daughters to complete such mundane chores.

First an apology. Now a helping hand. Who was this
Caleb Hutton?

And why did he catch her fancy?

Chapter 5

Caleb paid for his breakfast and few supplies, thanked Whitaker again for the tip about the livery and headed that way. He'd check with the blacksmith before he stopped at the printing office and the sawmill.

If given a choice, he'd take livestock over letters and lumber any day, though his life had been fairly equally divided between the first two.

The sprouting city sang with commotion, the street considerably more crowded than when he'd ridden in that morning. Hammers pounded from inside rising buildings, and freight wagons moaned beneath their burdens. Drivers whistled and cussed at their animals, and people on foot hurried along the boardwalks with apparent purpose.

And his purpose?

It wasn't washing dishes, that was for sure, but evidently his heart thought otherwise, for that's just what he'd done at the mercantile.

He grabbed his horses and led them toward the livery. What would Annie Whitaker think when she returned from unpacking and found the plates and cups drying on the sideboard? Would she see his efforts and wonder what they meant?

He sure enough wondered. Even Mollie Sullivan hadn't had this effect on him.

At the stable, he slapped dust from his hat and turned his back to the building across the road, grabbing hold of the last bit of optimism he could muster.

An oak of a man stood before a brick furnace at the back wall, sleeves rolled above massive forearms. One hand held tongs that gripped a glowing horseshoe atop a stump-mounted anvil, and the other hand wielded a hammer. The man lightly tapped the iron, then raised the shoe to appraise its shape and dunked the shoe in a bucket of water.

Caleb approached. "Mornin'," he said above the sound of the hissing bucket.

The smithy retrieved the dripping shoe, held it to the anvil and eyeballed Caleb. "Mornin'."

"Name's Caleb Hutton. Might you be Henry? Daniel Whitaker sent me round. Said you might be needing some help."

The leather-aproned man laid the hammer across the anvil and held out a blackened hand.

"I'm Henry Schultz. You know anything 'bout livery and stock?"

"Yes, sir," Caleb said. "Been around horses my whole life. Shod a few, birthed a few and trained even more."

Henry didn't release Caleb's hand but turned it over. "Looks mighty soft to me," he said. "Like a preacher."

At the word, Caleb flinched. Henry released his grip. Burning as if he'd touched the glowing iron instead of the man's hand, Caleb held Henry's gaze.

"It's been a while." His jaw tightened. "But I haven't forgotten. Just lost a few calluses."

Henry chuckled. "Well, if Whitaker sent you to me, I'll give you a try. I do my own shoein', but you can clean stalls and feed. Soap and mend the tack, and keep the freight drivers off my back." He jerked a thumb over his bearlike shoulders. "They park their wagons in the yard."

Caleb ran his hand around the inside of his hatband. The offer wasn't as alluring as cowboying all day, but it was work.

"Don't pay much, 'cause I don't got much."

Caleb was in no position to argue. "Whitaker mentioned a closed stall you lent out to someone else who moved on."

"That would be himself and his daughter."

The news surprised Caleb, but it explained Annie's refusal to let him help her unpack what he'd thought were stores. Rooms must be harder to come by in Cañon City than he thought if Whitaker was forced to board in a barn. Why hadn't they moved into the store to begin with?

Henry turned to the anvil, raised the hammer and pinged on the perfectly curved metal. "You're welcome to it, but it'll lower your pay by two bits a week."

"I'll take it."

Henry jerked his head toward the front. "First stall on the right. I'll throw in some straw for bedding, and you can put whatever you've got in there. You got a horse?"

"Two. But I can turn them out in your corral for the time being."

"That'll be fine. I'll deduct their feed from your pay, but they probably won't eat as much between the two of them as Whitaker's mare."

Caleb let himself smile. "That's what he told me. Asked if I'd take a look at her."

"Across the alley from your new room," Henry said.

"On the end." He dropped the shoe in a wooden box. "You start today?"

"Yes, sir."

"Good. Settle in and start on the stalls. Stock's all been fed this morning. Give them fresh water and hay at dusk. The pump's out by the corral."

Caleb nodded, put his hat on and left the barn with a lighter step. His eyes lit on the building across the road. When he saw the cross above the door, he nearly uttered a prayer of thanks. It would have been the first in a long time.

After dumping his tack and bedroll in the box stall, he led his animals around to the corral. Rooster trotted through the gate and kicked his heels, then dropped to the ground and rolled. Grateful, Caleb assumed, to be free of his burden.

He understood the feeling.

Inside the stable, Whitaker's mare watched him over the stall door and stuck her nose in his chest when he reached her.

"Looking for those apples, aren't you, girl?" Stepping inside the stall, he spoke softly, then rubbed her neck and withers. Her back was smooth and strong, not swayed, but her belly protruded on each side like a barrel. Suspicion urged his hands on, his fingers palpating, feeling for telltale knots.

She slapped her tail and reached back to nip his shoulder.

"It's all right, girl." He straightened and walked close around her hindquarters and up to her head, trailing his hand along her belly.

Whitaker wouldn't be any too happy with Caleb's findings. The man's yellow mare had about sixty days to go before she gave birth.

By the time he mucked out all the stalls, mended tack and fed the horses, late afternoon had tucked down behind the western peaks and shadows filled the livery. Tired but grateful for the sense of accomplishment in his aching back, he opened the door to his new home and stopped short.

Something sweet hung in the air, something that didn't belong in a horse barn. A perfumed soap or...

That was it. Annie.

He drank in the summery scent of Annie Whitaker's mahogany hair. She and her father had lived in this stall long enough to leave their mark.

Her mark.

He ignored the tightening in his chest as he felt along the walls for a lantern he'd seen earlier. He pulled a matchbox from his pocket and struck one against the lamp's base. The tiny flame threw shadows into the rafters and hayloft. He lifted the glass globe and held the match to the wick. Then he adjusted the wick and surveyed his lodgings.

A mound of fresh straw lay against the inside wall, and he spread it out and topped it with his bedroll. He hefted his saddle to the hayrack, and hung the bridle from the horn. The floor was surprisingly clean, and he smiled to himself. Annie Whitaker had taken her broom to it.

His stomach cried treason as he plopped onto his bedroll and dug through his saddlebags for the dried beef. Instead he found his Bible.

He'd once considered the book food for his soul. He thumbed through the pages and a thin copper casing fell to his lap. Mollie Sullivan's sweet face looked up at him. He slipped the image back between the pages of Jeremiah.

The weeping prophet. Appropriate place to hide the cause of his sorrows.

He set the Bible next to the lantern as a sudden rap on the stall door sent his hand to the Colt tucked inside his canvas.

"Caleb Hutton. You asleep?"

Caleb scrambled to his feet at Daniel Whitaker's call and

drew the door back. "Just settling in." He shoved the pistol into the back of his pants. Annie held a cloth-covered dish and a rich aroma curled before Caleb's face. Her father stood behind her.

"Hoped we'd find you here," Daniel said.

Caleb took the plate and his fingers brushed Annie's warm hands. "Thank you."

A shy smile curved her lips and she smoothed her apron. "We thought you could use a good meal."

"I appreciate it." More than he could say.

Her smile deepened and she stepped back.

"Looks like you made out all right with Henry," Daniel said.

"Yes, sir, thanks to your recommendation. Work and a roof over my head." Caleb glanced up into the open rafters and wondered again why the stable had once housed the Whitakers.

But it wasn't any of his business.

"Have a good night, son." Daniel motioned a farewell and turned toward the broad front door. Annie threw a quick glance toward the mare's stall and followed her father.

I know the thoughts that I think toward you.

The familiar words rose with the wonderful aroma, and a tightness gripped Caleb's chest as he closed the stall door. He sat on his bedroll, leaned against the wall and lifted the checkered cloth from the plate.

"Thank you," he said to no one in particular, laying the cloth in his lap. With relish, he grabbed the spoon buried in the thick stew and enjoyed the first real meal he'd had in weeks.

Pleased, though not completely satisfied, Annie stood in the center of the small storeroom, hands on her hips. She and her father had assembled the two rope beds they'd purchased in Denver and pushed one into each corner. Annie had unrolled a large braided rug and topped it with a small table, lamp and two chairs. A shelf against the back wall held a basin and pitcher and served as storage for their personal effects. And a camelback trunk hid their extra clothes and blankets and a few items from the hope chest she'd left behind.

Meager furnishings, indeed, but the beginnings of home.

"And you'd be thinking what, Annie?" Her father stood in the doorway, studying her thoughtful mood.

She reached to clasp his hands in hers.

"I'm thinking how much better this is than the stall at the livery." *And wondering how Caleb will fare at the barn.*

He looked around the room. "Almost like home, isn't it?"

"When we have a bigger table and a real cookstove, *then* it will be closer to home. But this space is too small for all that." A deep sigh escaped her. "Someday, we'll have a real house."

He squeezed her shoulder, then stepped into the room. "We'll be needing a curtain in the doorway for privacy during the day."

"I'll set out some canvas for Martha when she comes by tomorrow," Annie said. "I'm sure she can make us a curtain in no time with that fancy sewing machine of hers."

Her father coughed and rubbed a hand over his mouth. "What makes you think she'll be in tomorrow?"

"You know very well what." Annie picked up the folded quilt on her straw ticking and shook it out. "She's been in every morning since we got here—ever since she discovered what a handsome and eligible father I have."

His face suddenly reddened. "Confounded woman."

"Don't you mean confound*ing?*" Turning to hide a giggle, Annie retrieved two more quilts from the trunk, then handed one to her father. "That woman is taken with you, and I think you know it."

He huffed at her remark and sank onto his bed with a grunt.

"Don't let her get away, Daddy. She'd be good for you."

He met Annie's look with a worried frown. "Don't you go tryin' to marry me off. I don't need Martha Bobbins making my life more worrisome than it already is."

"Daddy, you've been alone for seventeen years. Don't you think it's time?"

Her father spread the quilt across the foot of his bed. "You're the one who should be looking for a beau, Annie. I've had my turn at life. And the good Lord has blessed me with two beautiful daughters and a good business. I've no need for anything else."

Her heart warmed to hear his tender words, but Annie could see that her father enjoyed Martha's attentions.

Annie, however, expected no man to call on her here in Cañon City—even if they did outnumber women six to one. Most had gold dust in their eyes or whiskey on their breath. Jedediah Cooper's flushed face materialized in her mind, and she shuddered.

"You're cold," her father said. "I'll stoke the fire. Give me your cover, Annie girl, and I'll hold it in front of the stove while you get ready for bed. And I'll warm up some bricks for bed warmers while I'm at it."

She handed him the eight-point star quilt, her favorite. He gave her a fatherly look.

"That Caleb Hutton showed himself a gentleman today, didn't he?"

Stunned by her father's obvious intentions, she fumbled with her hairpins.

"Why do you like him so much? Because he says 'sir' and 'ma'am' every other breath? We don't know anything about him other than they turned him away from the Lazy R. That might be a warning in itself."

Her father's brows raised. "Manners never did anyone any harm. And I believe that boy is honest and good."

"Well, I think he's hiding something. There's more to him than he's telling." She challenged her father's merriment. "And he's no boy. He's at least twenty-five."

Annie's left foot twitched as her father chuckled all the way to the stove, but she held it firmly to the floor and unfastened her shoes. After all their travels and living where nary a grass blade grew along the dusty streets, she'd worn the soles desperately thin. She had half a mind to order a pair of men's boots—if she could find them small enough. They were made so much sturdier than the thin-soled shoes women had to choose from.

What would Caleb Hutton think of her if he saw her stomping around Cañon City in men's boots?

Why did it matter what he thought? Annie chided herself as she shed her multiple skirts and petticoats and slid beneath the blankets. As she lay there, she recalled her room in Aunt Harriet's home. How often had she complained each summer in the thick, humid air that kept even a simple breeze from whispering through the open windows?

She tugged the blankets to her chin and gritted her teeth. She refused to pine away for that ornate home. Even if it did have a lovely fireplace in every bedroom and real bed warmers rather than hot bricks.

Before her father could return with her quilt, the day's labor conspired against Annie, and she drifted from her storeroom corner into the land of hopes and dreams. But even there, cold, crisp air brushed her face, and gold leaves fluttered against a bright blue backdrop.

Bundled against the autumn chill, she walked with a

basket of apples on her arm, approaching a stranger who stood before a small white church. He held his hat in his hands, and his dark head bent as if in prayer.

She touched the man's shoulder, and he looked up. With a start, she gasped at the pain on his face and drew back from the sorrow-filled eyes of Caleb Hutton.

Chapter 6

By sunup Caleb had all the stock fed and watered. His stomach had forgotten the previous night's hot meal, and he swung open the wide stable door and headed for the mercantile, in the hopes that Annie Whitaker was making fresh biscuits.

Keeping his eyes from the church across the road, he focused on the smoke curling from the mercantile rooftop, beckoning to him as his breath formed a white cloud in the air with every other step.

He now had a place to sleep, honest work and good food—much for which to be thankful. So why did he feel... cheated?

He dusted his hat against his leg, then stepped through the mercantile door to the chime of the bell. Annie stood at the back counter, and her father fed the stove. The aroma of fresh coffee vied with coal dust and the merchandise of a fully stocked store. It was a tableau he was beginning to count on, more than he wanted to admit.

"Mornin', Caleb," Whitaker said, grabbing another tin cup.

The brass bell rang a second time as he closed the door, and Annie looked over her shoulder. Caleb nodded a greeting, and she smiled briefly before returning to her work. The simple gesture set his heart to clanging as loud as that noisy bell.

He took the cup Whitaker offered and sat, trying not to look at Annie while he was talking to her father. It was harder than he would have thought.

"I'd say it's perfect timing." Whitaker took a seat and looked at his daughter. "We moved out of that stall yesterday morning and into the back of the store here—thanks to Annie's insistence that Jedediah Cooper rent the whole place to us, not just the front." One white brow raised in a crook and the other pointed toward his nose. "Not that I approve of her methods."

Looking unusually meek under her father's stern glance, Annie brought a large cast-iron skillet to the stove that brimmed with thick white gravy.

Caleb jumped up and reached for the skillet, sloshing coffee on his boots. "Let me help you."

"I have it," she said, turning the skillet from his reach. "No need to go spilling your coffee on account of this gravy."

Caleb watched her deftly handle the heavy skillet and center it on the small stove top.

"Smells mighty good, ma'am," he said, hoping he wasn't as pushy as his charges at the livery had been. He took his seat and caught a quiet laugh coming from behind Whitaker's raised tin mug.

Annie straightened and planted her small hands on her

hips, but this time her eyes held a friendly glint, unlike the double-edged sword he'd met yesterday morning.

"Do you like sausage gravy, Caleb?" A slight blush colored her cheeks at the use of his name. It made her look even prettier, if that was possible.

"I surely do. It's been a while since I had such fine cooking."

The remark raised her hand to her brow. She returned to the sideboard, set out three plates with biscuits and forks, then brought a ladle to the stove and stirred the gravy. "Won't be but a minute now," she said.

After serving, Annie took the only chair left—next to Caleb.

"Daddy, don't you think a prayer is in order, seeing as how we all have a place to live and food to eat?"

Caleb choked on the bite already in his mouth.

Annie shot a worried look his way. "You all right?"

He nodded, coughed a couple times and jerked beneath Whitaker's hearty back slap.

"You're not against praying are you, son?" The laughter in his voice assured Caleb that Whitaker was jesting.

"No, sir. Not at all." He pulled a bandanna from his hip pocket and wiped his mouth.

"Then why don't you do the honors?"

Caleb stared at the man. Did he see *preacher* written across Caleb's forehead?

Whitaker raised his silvery brows.

"Yes, sir," Caleb said. "Be happy to."

Annie dipped her head and folded her hands. Her father closed his eyes.

Caleb feared his heart would stop any moment and the others would be praying over his dead body instead of the biscuits and gravy. It had been a while since he'd offered up a prayer like this. He sucked in a deep breath and clamped his eyes shut.

"Lord...thank You." A familiar warmth invaded his chest as he forced his thoughts toward gratitude. "Thank You for this fine cooking and for the Whitakers' hospitality. And thank You for giving us all a roof over our heads and—" his voice bottomed out to a near whisper "—and for sending Your son, Jesus. Amen."

He opened his eyes to Annie staring at him as if he'd transformed right in front of her.

Which, in a way, he guessed he had.

"Amen to that, son," her father said. "Amen to that."

Caleb couldn't tear his eyes from Annie's, and his throat tightened at the tenderness he saw there. Something he'd never seen in Mollie Sullivan.

Annie paid little attention as she washed the skillet. Her mind kept replaying Caleb Hutton's prayer, and each time it stirred something in her that she shouldn't be feeling.

Not for a man she knew nothing about.

She peeked at him seated by the stove, scraping the last bit of gravy from his plate. There was more to this cowboy than he cared to let on, and she was determined to find out what it was. She dried her hands on her apron as her father hurried past without a word and out the back door, and Martha Bobbins rushed in beneath the singing bell.

"Good morning to you."

Annie shook her head at the woman's perpetual good nature, stuffed a handful of dried apples in her skirt pocket for later and greeted Martha at the front counter.

"You're here early." Annie noted how the crisp fall air had rouged Martha's cheeks, brightening her eyes to perfectly match the blue floral calico she wore.

"Martha, may I introduce you to Caleb Hutton?"

He stood with his hat in one hand and an empty plate in the other. "Ma'am." He nodded.

"Caleb, this is Martha Bobbins, our dressmaker in town and a good friend."

"Nice to meet you, Caleb." She scanned the store for its older proprietor, and her shoulders dropped the tiniest bit when she failed to find him.

"He's out back," Annie whispered with a conspiratorial grin.

The revelation brought a glow to Martha's already ruddy face, and she began an urgent search through her reticule. "I know my list is in here somewhere," she said.

Caleb slid his plate into the dishpan and retrieved his cup from the stove, where he stood tall and mysterious, sipping his coffee.

Annie's face warmed as she caught his eye, but she forced her thoughts to Martha's visit, pulled a bundle of heavy canvas from the shelves and unrolled a double length across the counter.

"Oh, no, child. I need lace. And buttons for Hannah's wedding dress."

"Yes, and I have some beautiful pearl buttons I'm sure you'll want. But before I fill your order, I have one of my own. I'm glad you came by."

Martha looked up, delight in her eyes.

"See the opening through the back wall, behind the stove? Daddy and I just moved in back there, and we need a curtain to draw during the day. I thought that might be an easy task for you with your sewing machine. Nothing fancy, just straight seams."

Martha patted Annie's hand. "Good for you. About time that old fox showed a little generosity." She picked up the cloth, giving Annie a chance to turn away and hide the hot blood that warmed her cheeks. Fox indeed. Wolf was more like it.

Caleb must have noticed her reaction for a questioning frown shadowed his face.

"A nice print would be more attractive, but this heavy canvas will do," Martha said. "I'll measure the opening and get started on it for you later today. Will that be soon enough?"

"Perfect," Annie said.

Martha moved toward the doorway just as Annie's father appeared.

"Oh, Daniel, dear. I'm so glad to see you." Martha seemed to coo. "Annie tells me you need a privacy curtain here for your new living quarters."

He coughed heartily, and Martha joined him in the back room as if she'd been invited.

Though she couldn't see him, Annie knew exactly how her father looked with his brows dipped to the bridge of his nose and his chin tucked in his chest.

"I know I have a tape measure in here somewhere," Martha said. "Yes, here it is. Daniel, hold this end for me while I take a measurement."

Caleb's boots sounded against the wood floor and he stopped at the counter. Annie busied herself refolding the fabric, trying to ignore his strong presence. She failed miserably and looked up into dark, worried eyes.

"Is your landlord less than a generous man?"

The question came low, for her ears only, and she sensed that Caleb's penetrating gaze would eventually pull the truth from her.

"Yes." She raised her chin, determined to hold her own against the likes of Jedediah Cooper. "But he has seen the error of his ways."

A question slid across Caleb's face, but the bell rang,

and a woman with two children entered. The little girl's eyes lit immediately on the licorice jar on the counter, and the boy, perhaps twelve, assumed a grown-up air until he recognized Caleb.

"Springer Smith." Caleb broke into a broad grin, so unlike his earlier worried expression that it took Annie by surprise.

The boy stuck out a hand and pulled off his floppy hat with the other. "Mr.…."

"Hutton," Caleb said, gripping the boy's proffered hand. "Caleb Hutton." He looked to the mother. "Mrs. Smith? Your son and I met a couple of evenings ago at the river."

Her concern vanished as she relaxed and cast a scolding eye at her son. "Yes, I do remember Ben mentioning a man camping downstream with his horses."

Caleb's demeanor warmed as he clasped the woman's hand with the slightest bow. "Good day, ma'am. I am sure you will find what you need here at the Whitaker's."

With that he disappeared through the door, leaving Annie marveling at his transformation.

More curious than ever, she wanted to follow the perplexing man and demand that he tell her who and what he was, but a customer awaited her.

Gathering her thoughts, she turned to the woman with a smile.

"What can I get for you?"

The woman pushed her bonnet back and loosened her cloak. "Have you heard of any rooms or cabins to rent?" Her bright cheeks betrayed a brisk walk, and from the sand that stuck to the girl's buttoned shoes, Annie guessed they were living at the river like so many people had during the summer. Like Caleb had?

"I'm Annie Whitaker." She came from behind the counter. The woman extended her cold hand. "Nice to meet you.

We're the Smiths. I'm Louisa, this is Emmy and that's Ben, or Springer, as he prefers, over there eyeing your leather goods."

"You have a lovely family, Louisa." Annie reached for the licorice jar and lowered her voice. "May I offer a welcome-to-town gift to the children?"

Louisa's lips thinned but quickly curved at Emmy's beseeching expression. "All right, but only one between them, please."

Overhearing the offer, Springer volunteered to divide the black whip in half. Annie held the jar toward him, and when he reached for a candy she playfully pulled it back. His startled eyes fastened on hers.

"If *you* break it in half, then your sister gets first choice."

He reached again, threw a glance at Emmy and snapped the candy in two. "You get to pick," he said, kneeling before his sibling.

Thrilled at getting to choose first, the child pulled the longest piece from her brother's fingers. "Thank you, Springer," she said, and leaned in to kiss him on the cheek.

"Thank Miss Whitaker, too, children," Louisa said with a laugh.

Springer nodded, grinning around the piece already in his mouth. "Thank you, ma'am."

"My pleasure." Annie bent toward Emmy. "I'm a younger sister, too, so I know we sometimes get the short end of the deal."

Emmy wrinkled her blond brow. "But I took the *long* one."

Springer laughed and returned to the saddles and horse blankets, and Emmy followed, giggling.

Annie straightened and faced Louisa. "There are so few places to live, but the Turk brothers are cutting timber in the Shadow Mountains this month and hauling logs for cabins. They made a trip last week, hoping to bring a sled full back before snowfall. If you'd like to leave them a note asking for a load, I have paper and pencil here."

The woman looked longingly at the crates of potatoes and apples and sifted a handful of dried beans through her fingers. "We're more likely to stay in our tent before we raise a cabin. I was hoping there might be an extra one with all the building I hear going on."

Annie's heart squeezed at the thought of keeping a family warm all winter in a tent.

Louisa spun slowly to survey the offerings. "Do you have stoves?"

"We have two ordered, and they should be in next week," Annie said. "They're small, not really cookstoves. More like the potbelly we have here in the store. But they're wonderfully warm, and if you plan it right, you can cook a good meal on one."

Louisa looked Annie in the eye with a smile. "Anything is an improvement to a campfire."

"How true." Annie was relieved to see good humor in the woman's expression.

"My William is a stonemason, and he's working for the Fairfax family. With the high demand for housing, he hasn't a moment to spare for cutting and fitting stones for our own home this winter. We'll just have to make do as best we can."

By the time the Smiths left with their purchases and an order for a few specialty items, Martha and Annie's father sat together near the stove. Relaxed and laughing, her father didn't see Annie studying him from behind the counter she pretended to dust.

She'd been right about them. They needed each other.

And what did she need?

Caleb Hutton's gentle voice settled on her heart like the yellow leaves that fell along the river.

That was what she needed. The river.

Her father and Martha could mind the store and enjoy a few moments alone.

"Martha, do you mind staying for a bit? I've an errand to run, and I hate to leave Daddy alone in case we're flooded with customers."

Her father stared, his mouth half-open. Martha rose with distinct pride at being needed. "I'd be happy to, dear." She fluttered her fingers toward Annie. "You run right along. We'll be fine."

Biting the inside of her mouth to keep a grin from breaking free, Annie stole a retreating glance at her father, who sat with one brow arched above a cutting glare.

"You're not going back—"

"No, Daddy. I promise." She'd not be visiting the Fremont Saloon ever again. She shivered as if shaking off the notion and saw again Caleb's questioning look. She tore a strip of brown paper from the large countertop roll and twisted two licorice pieces inside it. Then she escaped out the door before her father could say anything more.

Indian summer in Omaha was hot, muggy and hazy. In Cañon City it was warm, clear and sharp against a brilliant sky.

Last night she'd shivered in her bed, but today, the sun was brassy and warm, melting wintery thoughts and drawing birdsong from the woods. She lifted her face to a breeze, and cottonwood leaves trembled, gossiping as she passed.

A sudden whiff of beans assailed her, and Annie studied a tent cluster huddling in an open space ahead. Someone baked their evening meal with salt pork no doubt, for the aroma nudged her stomach into a whimper even though she wasn't hungry.

She turned downstream, continuing along the water's edge, mildly disappointed that the water merely chatted over rocky places. Where was the roaring white water of the mighty Arkansas? Where was the impassable raging river that gouged the Rocky Mountains?

A quick toss of her stockings and a hitch of her skirt, and she could wade right across without getting her knees wet. She paused, rolled the temptation around in her mind, imagining what it would feel like to tell Edna she'd done such a thing.

Childish laughter caught her ear, and she looked upstream. Springer and Emmy ran through the shallows near the tents, giggling and splashing water on each other.

She and Edna had never played like that. Edna had always been so proper, so ladylike, that her attitude goaded Annie to be as different as possible. And look where it had gotten her.

Alone in Kansas Territory—the farthest edge—with her father on the verge of finding companionship. Caleb's image rose in her mind's eye and her father's words slipped in beneath the water's happy murmur. *I believe that boy is honest and good.* What did Daddy know about Caleb? He was no boy, that was for sure. Good? Well, his prayer had sounded a chord in her heart that both pleased and disturbed her, making her almost doubt his honesty. She'd keep her own counsel on that until she knew more about the brooding horse handler.

Last night's dream had only added to the mystery.

But she had a feeling she was going to get to know more about Caleb soon.

A sudden honk and splashing lifted her gaze. Two Canada geese rose from a sandbar where others rested. Oh, the down ticking she could make from their soft undersides.

With a cautious glance around, she leaned against a large

boulder, stripped off her shoes and stockings and gathered her skirts. The water's icy caress pulled the breath from her lungs, and dozens of brown black-necked geese rose at her gasping intrusion, honking in protest.

No matter. They would return when she finished gleaning their "dead" feathers, and she'd ask a special blessing on their goslings when she snuggled beneath a new warm cover this winter.

After gathering a meager start on a feather ticking, she waded back through the icy river, clambered up the smooth granite boulder and wiggled her feet into her stockings and shoes.

As she approached Main Street, Jedediah Cooper exited the mercantile. She ducked back into the cross street and pressed against the barbershop wall, hoping he hadn't spotted her. Her hair would surely give her away. Why hadn't she worn a hat or scarf?

She shuddered. The saloon owner made her ill. He was not to be trusted, particularly by a woman alone, of that she was certain.

Peeking around the clapboard building's corner, she watched Cooper walk toward the saloon. Swagger, really, his bowler tipped to one side as if he owned all Cañon City and everyone should be grateful for it.

On her right stood the church building and directly across from it the livery. With a deep breath, she stepped from behind the building and crossed the wide street, praying Jedediah Cooper would not look in her direction as she made her way to talk with Caleb Hutton.

Chapter 7

Henry's hammer sang on the anvil as Caleb tossed straw into the big mare's stall. She'd cleaned her hayrack by the time he'd returned from breakfast, and now she lipped through the fresh bedding for stray oats in the mix. He needed to tell Daniel Whitaker about the horse's condition, but he suspected the storekeep would be less than happy about it.

Caleb leaned the pitchfork against the stall, stepped inside and kicked the straw around to spread it. "You need a few carrots from the mercantile. Don't you, girl?" He let her smell his hands and then rubbed them gently along her distended belly. "You going to make it to Christmas?"

As if in response to his question, a sudden kick pushed against his hand. The little hoof lay low toward the mare's hindquarters. Concern pulsed in Caleb's temple as he answered his own question.

"Too early to say, Mama. That baby could turn round

headfirst in no time. We'll just have to pray for the right delivery, won't we?"

There it was again—an old habit, resorting to prayer. This morning's prayer at breakfast had widened the hairline fissure, let something leak through. Resentment was draining away as sure as the green from the cottonwood leaves.

"Forgive me, Lord," he whispered. He tipped his forehead against the mare's neck and pulled his fingers through her mane. "Forgive me for being so stubborn and hardhearted. I don't deserve anything more than a bed in a barn, after turning my back on You."

A scuffling step jerked his head up. Annie Whitaker stood watching him, her face flushed, eyes wide. As she approached, her eyes softened and warmed, drinking in the scene. Her lips parted to speak but instead curved slightly as she slipped a hand over the stall gate and let the mare lip her open palm with a low whinny.

Caleb ducked beneath the horse's neck and when Annie stepped back, he exited the stall.

"I knew she'd be missing the apples," Annie said.

He stood close to her, against the closed gate. Her hair, mere inches from his face, enticed him with its sweet fragrance.

She dug in her pocket again and this time offered Caleb the wrapped licorice whips.

He grinned. "Why, thank you, ma'am."

Her brows pulled together. "I told you, it's Annie. You make me feel like an old woman every time you say 'ma'am.'"

His fingers brushed against her palm, and he immediately wanted it to happen again. "Annie." He popped a piece into his mouth and offered one to her.

She shook her head, and he could smell the sunshine in her hair again. "Those are for you. I have my own."

"Deep pockets," he said.

She caught the jest in his voice. "Only for apples and licorice."

"So you're barely making it, like everyone else around here, I expect." He bit into another strip. "Except maybe the owner of the Fremont Hotel and Saloon."

She stiffened at his remark and he faced her straight on. "What's wrong, Annie?"

The rose in her cheeks had all but faded, and she pushed at the loose hair falling so appealingly against her neck. "What do you think of Nell?"

Her sudden change in tone and subject convinced him that he was right—that there was a problem with Cooper—but her lovely eyes focused on the mare.

"Is that her name?" he said. "Nell?"

"Mmm-hmm." Annie nodded and rubbed the horse's head.

"You were right about her eating more than the others," he said, trying to figure out how to politely mention the fact that the mare would be foaling within two months.

"Do you know why?"

His hand itched to stroke Annie's cheek, finger her russet locks. Instead he gripped the gate and watched the horse that stood half dozing under Annie's loving attention. "Yes, I believe I do."

Annie raised her beautiful eyes to him.

He cleared his throat. One hand rubbed the back of his neck. "Well, uh…"

His hesitation made her frown, and worry darted across her face.

"Is Nell all right?" She placed her hand atop his on the

rail. "Is something the matter with her? We didn't take care of our horses in Omaha, someone else did. Have we done something wrong?"

"No, nothing's *wrong*." How should he put it? And how could he speak calmly with her hand on his in such an earnest, trusting gesture? He squeezed the rail and took a deep breath. "She's eating a lot because she's not the only one getting her food." He watched to see if Annie gathered his meaning.

Her eyes flicked from his face to the mare and back again, and he saw the exact moment realization settled. With a gasp she jerked her hand away and covered her mouth.

"You mean…"

He nodded. "My guess is sometime around Christmas. You didn't know?"

Light danced in her eyes, and her mouth bowed into a perfect circle. "Oh—that's wonderful." She leaned over the half door and kissed Nell on the nose. "You old darling. What a Christmas surprise you've brought us."

Relief spilled out with Caleb's pent-up breath. "At least your father will be surprised."

His comment brought back her frown. "You are right about that." She turned her back to the stall and leaned against the railing, folded her arms across her waist and gave him a calculating look.

Caleb knew conspiracy when he saw it.

"We can't tell him," she said. "Promise me you won't let him know. He'll sell her for sure, and it just wouldn't be fair, not when she's in a family way—" A becoming flush appeared on her cheeks, and she pushed away from the stall and paced the alleyway.

"It's not going to be a secret for very much longer," he said. "If he comes down here, he's bound to figure it out."

She stopped and studied Henry at his fire in the back of the barn. Then she whirled on him.

"Are you a veterinarian?"

Annie Whitaker didn't sashay around the point. If he wasn't careful, she'd drag every ounce of his past right up through his gullet.

"No." He reached for the pitchfork.

"Then what are you?"

He walked back to the straw pile and forked a load, stalling for time and a decent answer. He wasn't about to start lying, but he wasn't ready to admit he'd turned from his calling, either.

"I told you. I'm good with horses." He tossed the straw into the stall farthest from his inquisitor and stabbed the tines in the ground at his feet. Then he crossed his own arms and waited, daring her to press the issue further.

Annie narrowed her eyes. She'd heard Caleb Hutton asking forgiveness for something, so what was it? Was he hiding some terrible deed and lying to them. One thing she knew for sure: he was as stubborn as Edna ever had been. By his rigid chin and the wide stance of his feet, she guessed he had a passel of younger brothers and sisters and knew all the tricks to avoiding a direct question when he didn't want to give the answer.

His broad shoulders and steady gaze nearly weakened her determination, but she averted her eyes just in time. She had more important things to consider than his disarming looks. She needed a vet for Nell, or at least someone who knew what to do when the time came.

He may not be an animal doctor, but Caleb Hutton knew more than he was letting on. Much more than a livery hand, or horse handler, or whatever he chose to say about himself. *Still water runs deep,* Daddy had said a hundred times.

If that was true, she was squared off against a bottomless ravine.

Nell stomped and pulled Annie's attention from the mysterious man in the alleyway. How did he know so much about horses? And how did he connect to the sorrowful Caleb in her dream? Suddenly she wasn't quite sure who she was talking to. That feeling of suspicion about Caleb Hutton arose in her again.

Annie scoured her pockets and found two more apple rings. Nell lipped them from her palm and nestled her nose against Annie's shoulder. "You poor dear," she cooed. "Don't you worry. We'll find someone to help you."

"I don't think she's worried," Caleb said. At that instant, Nell tossed her head, nudging Annie off balance. She stumbled back into a hard chest and strong hands—the second time in as many days she'd found herself thrust into a man's arms.

Only this time, she had to admit, was much more… pleasant. The very thought made her feel even more off balance.

"Whoa, there," Caleb said, laughter edging his voice.

"Thank you, but I'm perfectly capable of standing on my own." Gathering her footing and her pride, she fisted her hand around her pocketed clutch of goose down.

His expression quivered with mirth.

Her left foot itched to stomp the hard-packed dirt, but she held it firm. "I need to get back to the store. Daddy will worry if I'm gone too long."

She stepped around him and refused to look up until she reached the livery door.

"You won't tell him, will you?" she asked over her shoulder.

"No," he said, his mouth knit up in that ridiculous lopsided grin. "I won't tell him. But Nell will, eventually."

Annie huffed and jerked her head around, dislodging her hair. A thick strand fell over her shoulder and she hurried through the wide doorway, refusing to stoop for the traitorous pins.

Once she made it past the corral, she glanced back to see Caleb bent over, picking up the pins from the dirt. He caught her eye before she looked away and escaped to the boardwalk.

By the time she reached the mercantile, Annie had fumed up enough steam to wilt an entire garden of Aunt Harriet's daylilies. She knew no more about Caleb Hutton than she did before her visit to the livery. She slammed the door harder than she intended, and her father's and Martha's shocked expressions warned her to calm her billowing emotions.

Caleb Hutton's stubbornness was stouter than her father's coffee. She paused, looked out through the door glass and drew in a slow, deep breath. She mustn't give away Nell's secret. Not yet.

"I must be going, Daniel." Endearment flavored Martha's tone. "Thank you for the coffee and company. You've done my heart a world of good."

Annie forced herself to walk calmly to the back wall. Her father offered Martha his hand and smiled as the little woman stood and faced him.

"You are a dear," she said. Then she gathered the folded canvas and her reticule and addressed Annie.

"I didn't get my lace and buttons, but I'll be back tomorrow with your curtain."

Guilt wedged under Annie's festering irritation, and she burned with chagrin. "I apologize. I shouldn't have been gone so long."

Martha fluttered her fingers over her shoulder on her way to the door. "I shall return, dear." She paused and sent a secret look to Annie's father. "For more of that coffee, Daniel. I may even find some cinnamon rolls while I'm rummaging around my kitchen."

The bell sang much more sweetly upon Martha's departure than it had at Annie's arrival. She regarded her father's changed countenance. What had transpired while she was gone? He was as peaceful as she was agitated.

"Daddy?"

He stood with his hands clasped behind his back, rocking onto his toes, deep in thought.

"Daddy?" She moved closer and touched his arm.

"Annie, girl, you may have been right after all."

Fear suddenly skipped from her stomach into her heart, surprising Annie. She wasn't ready for her father to make any sudden changes—in spite of what she'd said earlier. It was enough that they'd uprooted and moved to Cañon City.

"Daddy, what happened here?"

His eyes twinkled with a secret, and Annie's pulse quickened. One secret between them was enough, especially when it was *her* secret. She planted her hands on her hips and assumed her most commanding posture.

"Daddy, what are you talking about? What's going on between you and Martha?"

Exactly like Caleb had earlier, her father turned his back on her. He reached into the coal bucket, opened the stove door and planted two small pieces inside. It wasn't even cold in the store. After closing the door and adjusting the damper, he addressed her with controlled grace. "I enjoy her company, that's all."

He walked purposefully to the front counter.

"She's a fine woman, that Martha. A fine woman."

Yesterday Martha Bobbins had been a "confounded woman." Today she was "fine."

That left Annie as the confounded one—confounded over the feelings growing in her heart for one mysterious cowboy.

Chapter 8

Caleb shoved the pitchfork beneath a soiled straw pile and tossed it onto the wheelbarrow. Pungent warmth rose from the heap.

November nights had been considerably colder, but by sunup each day he worked up a sweat cleaning stalls and tossing hay from the loft. And if Henry had the fire stoked and blowing, it felt like near summer in the livery by noon.

The last time he'd been to the river, he'd found ice forming along the banks and Springer Smith treading dangerously close to it. He hoped the family had better shelter by now, something more than a campfire and a tent. Wintering along the Arkansas would be unbearable.

Cañon City needed a boardinghouse, someplace where families or single men could afford to stay.

Like himself.

He moved to the next stall, raked out what needed to be raked and added it to the wheelbarrow. *Thank You,*

Lord, for warmth and work and good food each morning at Whitaker's Mercantile.

Annie's image came to mind, as it did so often now. He laughed aloud at the ire he'd raised in her by refusing to give her any information about himself.

He was doing it again—thinking about Annie when he'd told himself not to.

Truth was, *everything* brought Annie to mind. Just the thought of her drew him like a bear to a beehive—a dangerous delight. No matter what he did, his mind's eye envisioned Annie Whitaker with her flaming hair and luminous eyes and persistent questions about his past.

The woman pressed in where she had no right to go.

He dug into the pile of fresh straw in the alleyway and sent a heaving pitch against the far wall and all over one of Deacon's draft horses. Caleb shook his head and jabbed the fork in the dirt, then climbed in to brush off the big gray horse.

So why didn't he simply tell her the truth?

Because it's none of her business.

The horse stood calmly as Caleb pulled straw pieces from its thick mane. The irony of his work set his teeth on edge. Sunday or not, the animals required care and their needs came before his.

He stepped through the gate and looked to Henry's furnace staring from the end of the alleyway, cold and empty. The anvil lay dutifully quiet on this day of rest for everyone except the former preacher.

The past two weeks Caleb had slipped into the church after the singing and stood near the door, ready to bolt if confronted. Reverend Hartman was near his own age, and his straightforward sermons rang a familiar note. It was almost a comfort.

Both Sundays Caleb had left during the closing prayer

and managed to avoid Hartman, the Whitakers and Martha
Bobbins, who clung to Daniel's arm like a foxtail to a dog.
But today he planned to stay and face the fire.

The fire of repentance or the fire in his heart for Annie—
he wasn't sure which.

He hung the pitchfork on the wall and hauled in water
from the hand pump. His new basin and pitcher rested on
an upturned crate in his stall, and he washed his hands and
face. He changed into his clean pants and shirt, thankful
that he'd stopped by the barber's the day before for a haircut.

If he wasn't careful, gratitude might become a habit.

He reached for his Bible and found the passage he'd read
last night by lamplight. *Wither shall I go from thy spirit?*
or whither shall I flee from thy presence?

An honest question that Caleb hadn't been willing to
answer.

He couldn't hide from God forever. Not even in Cañon
City, at the edge of nowhere. It'd be a long winter if he kept
running from the church folk in town, especially since he
wanted to get a lot closer to one in particular.

Clattering hooves, creaking buggy wheels and the curious snorts of his stablemates told him people were gathering across the road. His gut twisted, anticipating Annie
Whitaker fresh as a spring flower in her Sunday dress and
bonnet.

He buttoned his waistcoat, dusted off his hat and walked
the line for one last check. Nell dozed with a back leg
cocked forward, her distended belly looking painfully tight.
There could be two inside—double the problem if Annie
was right and her father wanted nothing to do with another
horse to feed. He brushed his shirtsleeves and wished he
had a nicer overcoat than his duster. The chill nipped clean
through his thin shirt, but he couldn't wear his work coat
to the meetinghouse. They'd run him off for sure.

A woman's clear laughter sang from the boardwalk. Annie? He hurried through the doors to spot the source of the melodic sound, something deep within him insisting it must be her.

Annie walked beside her father, her head tilted back in an unguarded moment. Daniel wore a grin beneath his white mustache and a smiling Martha Bobbins on his arm.

The threesome stepped into the street, and Annie hitched up her deep green skirt as they crossed, revealing high buttoned shoes and an unintended glimpse of dark stockings. Caleb's chest warmed with a flash, and his need for a coat vanished.

"Mornin'." Henry Schultz's hearty welcome caught Caleb staring.

"Henry." He pulled on his hat brim. "Mrs. Schultz, ma'am."

He fell in with the couple as they made their way up the steps and waited behind them when they stopped before the pastor.

Hartman stood at the door, greeting each congregant individually, and he offered his hand to both Henry and his wife.

"Good to see you this morning. Bertha, don't you look lovely." An honest smile accompanied his words, and he shared one with Caleb, as well. "You're early." Laughter sparked in the parson's gray eyes.

Caleb pulled off his hat and took the pastor's hand. "Thought I'd sit in on the whole service this morning."

Hartman slapped Caleb's arm. "I'm glad to hear I haven't driven you off."

Henry offered seating at their usual bench, but Caleb begged off on the pretense of keeping an eye on the stable and slid into the back row. He wasn't quite ready to be so close to the pulpit.

And the view was a bit better from the back row.

Henry bent and lowered his voice. "I do believe you're keeping an eye on more than the livery."

Caleb hadn't realized he was so obvious.

Bertha pulled on Henry's arm, and Caleb pulled on his collar, pretending for himself as much as for anyone else that it was the chapel's woodstove putting out so much heat that had caused his face to redden.

Annie had seen Caleb exit the livery. She wanted to cross to him right then and there and tell him that she knew he was hiding something, that there was something he wasn't saying.

And it wasn't just their secret about Nell.

But ladies did not run after men in public, or anywhere, for that matter. She straightened her spine and tried to ignore the irritation she felt as she recalled Caleb's tight-lipped responses to her questions.

It just wasn't that easy to ignore anything having to do with Caleb. How handsome he was this morning—his long, confident stride, his clean white shirt, his low, tilted hat. Could he be the same man that had taken a stubborn stance and refused to answer her questions?

At the steps she paused to let her father and Martha go ahead. Once inside she angled away from the door, tucked her Bible under an arm and fussed with her reticule as she listened to Caleb's deep voice while he spoke to Pastor Hartman.

When he passed by, she turned and fingered a stray lock beneath her velvet hat, then stepped in behind a young couple heading down the aisle. From behind her raised hand, she peeked at the horse handler seated on the last bench, broad hat in his hands, an inscrutable expression on his face.

During the sermon it took all her concentration to focus

on the message. Her mind wandered—daydreams about who and what Caleb could be interrupted Reverend Hartman's sermon on the parable of the sower.

A hired gun? He wore no holster.

A grieving widower? He wore no ring.

A swindler, a bank robber, a gambler?

She snickered, and her father cocked an eyebrow her way. Quickly she seamed her lips, a childhood trick she'd used when hiding a joke from Edna. But it wasn't enough to keep her thoughts where they should be. Her mind kept returning to Caleb.

The man had all but finished off an entire apple pie on one visit to the store. He ate more than she and her father put together. Perhaps he was a farmer, missing his fields and family back home. Had he come for a share of fertile land in the Arkansas River Valley and been robbed?

Everyone stood, and Annie rushed to her feet, heat flooding her face. The closing song forced her attention to the blessed tie that binds, but during the prayer she finally gave in to her desire to peek over her shoulder. She couldn't make Caleb out through all the bowed heads. Either his was also bowed or, like before, he'd slipped out already. The binding tie pulled to a disappointed knot.

"You must come for dinner, dear," Martha said, gripping Annie by the elbow as they drifted out the chapel door when the service was over. "I've made a chicken pie and a lovely rice pudding for desert."

Annie looked to her father, whose eyes fairly brimmed with longing for both, she guessed.

Laughing, she linked her arm with the little woman. "Of course we will come. Can we bring anything from the mercantile? Tea or coffee?"

"No, I have everything. But we'll need to hurry. I left the pie on the back of the stove to keep warm."

Just then, Hannah Baker, Cañon City's bride-to-be, caught Martha's eye as they exited the church. So much for hurrying.

Wanting for her heart's soil to be fertile and not futile, Annie resisted an envious tug. Fair Hannah could not be more than sixteen, yet here she was, engaged to be married to Reverend Hartman. An Abraham and Sarah romance, no doubt. Or was romance even involved?

Annie watched the animated girl describe to Martha the precise placement of seed pearls that she wanted on her gown. Her flushed cheeks and the urgency in her voice betrayed a deep and earnest passion.

Envy took a step closer, but Annie backed away.

While Hannah bombarded Martha, Annie's father ambled over to visit with Henry and Mrs. Schultz. Annie's breath froze in her chest.

What if Henry mentioned Nell's condition?

She couldn't bear to sell the mare now, not like this. Not with winter coming on and long, dark nights ahead. *Oh, Lord, please.*

"He won't say anything."

Annie whirled to face the man who had read her thoughts and answered her unspoken prayer.

Trying to find her breath, she fingered the cameo broach at her throat.

"Are you sure?" she whispered, clutching her Bible to her chest.

One side of his mouth twitched as if he fought a smile.

"He might not even know." Caleb lowered his head, holding her with his eyes. "He doesn't pay the horses much mind."

Annie pulled in a deep breath. Was it fear of discovery or the intimacy of Caleb's rich voice that left her light-headed?

"Oh, I pray you're right."

A muscle flexed in his jaw, and his eyes swept her face, making her dip her head to avoid his gaze. Where was the anger that she'd last felt in his presence?

She pushed at the small hat clinging desperately to her hair. He held out his opened hand, revealing two hairpins. "Looking for these?"

She met his gaze and saw nothing but gentleness. No mockery, no criticism. She reached for the pins, and as her fingers brushed his palm, he clasped her hand in his.

"Truce?"

The warmth of his strong hand drew the very breath from her.

She nodded, helpless to do more, and he released her fingers as quickly as he had closed upon them.

"Come along, dear," Martha piped from the church steps. "And you, too, young man. There's chicken pie aplenty to go round. You know what they say—the more the merrier."

Annie's Sunday suit squeezed tightly as she fought for a steadying breath. Now she was forced to share much more than a truce with the man. And not just casual biscuits around a potbellied stove, but an intimate meal with Martha and her father.

Caleb offered his arm. For three beats of his heart, he watched indecision cloud Annie's eyes. When she finally rested her fingers in the crook of his elbow, his pulse nearly broke and ran. With one hand, she again lifted her skirt as they crossed the dusty street, and he fought the urge to sweep her into his arms and carry her across.

As they passed the Fremont Saloon, Annie tensed, raised her chin and stared straight ahead. The others walked by the ornate doors with no response. What had Jedediah Cooper done to make Annie react so strongly to even the man's establishment?

At the next corner, they strolled north, and Martha led them to a rock-lined path and a small cabin with a stone chimney. White lace curtains peeked through the front window, clinging to their place against the rough logs that framed them.

"Come in, come in," Martha said, holding the door wide with a smile to match.

The aroma of baked chicken and piecrust set Caleb's mouth to watering, and the amply supplied table vied with church dinners he'd long forgotten.

An unusual contraption hugged one wall, draped in long, silky folds with silver pins along an unsewn edge. Martha's latest project.

A large braided rug covered the tiny cabin's floor, but by Caleb's living standards, the homey room was a palace.

He hung his hat on a peg by the door and noted that Martha had set the table for three in expectation of the Whitakers. She whisked an additional plate and utensils from the sideboard, quickly balanced the small round table for four and insisted everyone be seated.

"Thank you, ma'am," Caleb said. "I'm hungry as a horse."

"Speaking of horses, Caleb," Daniel said, "have you noticed anything unusual about our mare that would keep someone from buying her?"

Annie choked on the morsel in her mouth.

Caleb's heart twinged at the barbed look she threw him over her napkin. So much for their truce. Her heart would break if her father sold Nell, especially with the foal on the way. And she would blame him.

He rested his hand at the table's edge. "Why sell her, sir?"

Daniel harrumphed around a mouthful, then swallowed. "Well, I'm sure at this point, Caleb, that you've seen how much she eats."

Caleb glanced from Daniel to Annie's warning glare and back.

"I suspect it'd be hard to sell her now, so close to the snow coming. You might get a better price if you wait until spring."

Daniel chewed on Martha's chicken and Caleb's reply, his white brows pulled together. "Duke Deacon said he'd think on buying her."

Annie's head snapped toward her father. "We can't sell her." She seemed to catch herself, dabbing her mouth with her napkin and softening her tone. "Did the freighters really say they wanted her?"

Daniel's tender glance at his daughter eased the creases at his eyes. He shook his head. "I know you love her, though why, I'll never understand. But she's too expensive a pet, Annie girl. And she's built for pulling a load."

Martha eyed her guests and diverted the approaching storm. "Wasn't that a most uplifting sermon this morning?" She winked at Caleb. "What did you think, Daniel?"

The man's countenance softened further as his eyes met Martha's. "Indeed it was. Love your neighbor as yourself."

"That wasn't it at all." Annie huffed and balled her napkin. "It was the parable of the sower."

Daniel laughed, and his belly bumped the table's edge. "So it was, Annie. So it was."

Martha flushed pink and worried a chicken piece on her plate. Things had definitely changed between Annie's father and the seamstress, and Caleb wondered if Martha would be changing her name as easily as she'd changed the topic of discussion.

His gaze shifted to Annie, who stared at a spot on the white tablecloth above her plate. Her fitted green jacket set off her hair in flaming contrast, and two tortoiseshell combs held it off her face, exposing the tender skin at her temples.

"There's plenty more," Martha said, lifting Daniel's empty plate.

"Don't mind if I do," he said.

Martha heaped on creamy chicken and vegetables, then reached for Annie's plate.

"No, thank you," she said, returning from her reverie. "It was wonderful. Really quite good, but I dare not eat another bite." She pressed one hand against her narrow waist as she tucked her napkin beneath her plate. "It's so nice outdoors, I think I'll walk through the garden while you and Daddy finish."

Martha waved a hand. "Oh, it's hardly a garden. Just a few rosebushes that attract more deer than honeybees."

Annie scooted her chair back and took her plate to the sideboard.

"Believe I'll do the same," Caleb said, sensing a rare opportunity to talk to Annie alone. "Again, thank you, ma'am. This was a fine feast."

Martha tilted her head modestly. Caleb noticed that her fingers had already found their way to Daniel's free hand lying conveniently near her on the table, despite the fact that he and Annie had not left the room yet.

Caleb set his plate atop Annie's in the dishpan and quickly followed her outside, anxious to apologize to her once again.

Chapter 9

Annie looked up from a fading rose at the cabin's corner to see Caleb making his way toward her, a sober look on his face.

"I'm sorry," he said.

She shook her head and turned back to the rose, plucking at the dying petals.

"It's not your fault." Her finger snagged on a thorn, drawing a red bead at the tip. Squeezing her finger, she commanded the tears that pricked her eyes to hold their place.

Caleb reached for her hand, unpocketed a red bandanna and held it against the wound.

Feeling foolish for such a careless act, Annie tried to pull away, but he held her fast—firmly, yet gently. His eyes roamed her brow, her cheeks, her lips, as if charting every inch of her face. A flutter caught in her throat, and she feared that she matched the rose's once deep pink.

"I could have said *bear*."

Curious, she tipped her head.

"I could have said I was hungry as a bear."

Laughter eased the tightness in her shoulders, and she relaxed her hand in his. He continued to hold it, though she was fairly certain the bleeding had stopped.

"It's not your fault. Daddy has wanted to be rid of Nell for a long time, but I don't want to let her go. I love her soft breath on my face, the way she nuzzles me for the apples…"

Catching herself, Annie withdrew her hand and looked away. What was it about Caleb Hutton that made her want to trust him with such personal details? Feeling exposed, she regretted leaving her hat indoors and nervously fingered the new combs in her hair. And yet she kept talking.

"We left everything familiar back home, and when we bought the horses in Denver, it was as if our traveling family expanded. I had more to care for than just myself and my father."

She clasped her hands at her waist. "How could I have known that she was…"

The heat of embarrassment flooded her neck.

"I'll talk to those freighters the next time they come to the wagon yard. Spring is the time for buying a horse. They're not making many trips out until then anyway."

She peeked at his face. Why had she never before noticed the depth of his dark eyes?

He stuffed the bandanna back in his pocket and, offering his arm, gestured toward the narrow lane. "Care to walk?"

She hooked her fingers in his elbow and allowed him to lead her away from the rosebushes and toward the path.

They strolled up the lane, away from town, and warmth spread from his strong arm into hers. Wood smoke painted the breeze and falling leaves laid an amber carpet at their feet.

Caleb cleared his throat and threw her a sidelong glance. "Which is worse?" he asked her. "Telling your father about the coming foal before it arrives or waiting until it gets here?"

A heavy sigh slipped out. "I've asked myself the same thing a hundred times. I'm just afraid."

He stopped abruptly, surprise and doubt in his scrutiny. "I find that hard to believe, you of the broom and the biscuits."

His boldness startled a laugh where once it would have elicited a scowl. "You are taking a fearsome chance with that remark, Mr. Hutton. A fearsome chance."

Placing his free hand atop hers on his arm, he resumed their stroll. "I can't imagine you being afraid of anything on this earth, Annie Whitaker. I've seen a fire in your eyes that I'm certain lies deeply banked within your heart."

Poetry? Annie doubted if her sister's beaus spun words as well as this cowboy at her side.

But he wasn't a beau. At least, he wasn't *her* beau.

Befuddled, she studied the ground. Her right hand burned hotter than her left, covered as it was by his calloused fingers. Strength flowed from him—steadily, faithfully, as if he drew on some hidden source. His prayer so long ago at the mercantile suggested an intimate knowledge of God. Did he share her faith?

Each time they were together, something new came to her attention—his humility, candor, humor. What *was* he? Saddle tramps didn't talk like that—or pray like that. This man had a "way" with more than just horses.

What was he hiding?

"Have you been upstream?"

Caught in her puzzlement, she took a moment to reorient. "Upstream?" She cocked her head to look up at him. "As in upriver?"

Amusement stretched his mouth to one side. "Yes, up-river. Have you ridden up the river, into the canyon above town?"

"Not yet," she said, unable to hide the surprise in her voice. Caleb was referring to the very thing she'd looked forward to in Cañon City. But as far as she could see, the Arkansas River didn't roar any more than the lazy Mississippi, at least not near town.

"I plan to take some time off tomorrow—if we don't get any new freighters—and ride up past the Ute encampment. Take a look at the canyon the town is named for."

Envy danced across her mind like a Paris cancan girl. Once again, a man had the freedom to do something *she* wanted to do.

"Daddy says the canyon narrows down to the width of the river. At least that's what someone told him."

Her responsibilities at the mercantile gave her little free time before dark, and only a fool ventured out at night. But even during the day, Daddy would never let her ride unattended. Neither would he take time off from the store to ogle the scenery.

Caleb cast a questioning look her way. Evidently her hidden frustration was not so hidden.

"When you get back, you'll have to tell me all about it."

"I'd be happy to. Or, if it's not too treacherous, I'll take you up for a look. That is, if your father wouldn't mind."

She'd not come to Cañon City to have her head turned by a wandering cowboy with no home or livelihood, she reminded herself. But she *had* come to hear the mighty river roar.

Lifting her chin to a dignified angle, she skimmed every eager note from her voice and aimed for detached and demure. "How delightful, but I'd have to wait until after Nell…"

Caleb stopped and faced her. "You could ride Sally."

"Excuse me?" She eased her hand from his arm and hid it safely in the folds of her skirt.

"My spare mount." Amusement lit his eyes. "She's a gentle old girl and would serve you well."

"Oh." Uncertain how she felt about him practically laughing at her and confused about what the right thing was to do, Annie turned back the way they had come.

In one long stride, he fell in beside her. "I've had Sally since I was a boy. My pa gave her to me, and she's been a faithful horse. Never bucked or bit and fared better on the trip here than I had hoped."

Unpredictable didn't begin to describe Caleb Hutton. Now the tight-lipped loaner was spilling history with a schoolteacher's flair.

Annie stopped and faced him. He wasn't the only one full of surprises. "Thank you for your kind offer to ride Sally on a river excursion. I think that is a splendid idea."

That night Caleb lay with his hands linked beneath his head, his lamp trimmed low, ignoring the barn cat meowing at the stall door.

He mulled over the pastor's morning message, picking through the seeds he'd sown in the past five years. Not much had sprung from his meager plantings and yet the quiet walk with Annie had set his heart to galloping and his dreams to spinning. But what did he have to offer a beautiful woman with mahogany eyes? A box stall in a livery stable?

He saw again the warm parsonage he'd left in Missouri. And Mollie Sullivan—far from warm as he compared her now to Annie. He'd had a calling and a home when he'd lost Mollie to someone of greater means.

He was a fool to think Annie would give him a second thought.

A light scratch lifted his attention to the rafters, where a black-and-white feline walked the crossbeam like a high-wire performer. Without a sound, it leaped to the railing along the wall and dropped to the floor.

He chuckled as she neared his bedroll.

"Won't the horses let you sleep with them?"

She purred against his hand and pressed her head into his rough blanket. He missed the heavy quilts back in the parsonage, the colorful spreads pieced together by the Women's Society. He'd never properly thanked them for their labors—another shortsighted sin.

He'd thought only of himself in Saint Joseph. Of marrying the prettiest girl in the congregation, of listing converts beneath his name, of counting the people who sat in the walnut pews of his sanctuary.

His sanctuary. Not the Lord's.

He grimaced at his arrogant attitude.

When had he fallen from serving God to serving himself?

The cat curled into a ball at his side and wrapped her tail around her face. He stroked her back, ran his fingers through her soft fur.

"Forgive me, Lord," he murmured. "Give me another chance—tell me what to do. Not just for a warm hearth and a woman's love, but for You. I'll stay in this barn if it's what You want. Just show me what to do, how to get back to the place I should be."

He reached toward the crate and trimmed the lamp until the wick smoked out, then rolled to his side. He closed his eyes and soon drifted across a ripening wheat field, golden heads bent beneath a scuttling breeze. He saw himself running through the field—running toward an aging man who stood open-armed, tears streaming down his face and into his beard.

Caleb fell at the man's feet but was embraced and lifted upright.

And after that, Caleb dreamed no more, but slept as soundly and deeply as he ever had.

By the time Caleb broke ice on the water trough, fed the horses and made his way to the mercantile the next morning, a crowd had already gathered around the potbellied stove. He removed his hat and stepped into the boisterous group helping themselves to Martha's fresh cinnamon rolls and arguing the merits of the recently elected president. Had he been in the states and not on the frontier, Caleb would have cast his vote as a citizen ought.

"Lincoln won by a landslide," said Jeb Hancock, a tall freighter from Illinois. His chest swelled more than the last time he'd been in the livery.

"Yesiree, got us a good 'un this time," Hancock boasted.

A stumpy miner jostled to the front and grabbed two rolls. His crumpled hat and ragged canvas coat bore witness to a played-out claim.

"It's the end, I tell ya, the end." The miner shoved one roll in his mouth and the other in his pocket and headed for the door.

"Good riddance," Hancock called over those who crowded the stove. "Naysayer." He swiped his buckskin coat sleeve across his mouth and downed his coffee dregs.

Annie stood at the back counter watching the commotion with concern. When Caleb caught her eye, she brightened and seemed to relax. Or was he just seeing what he wanted to see?

It certainly wouldn't be the first time.

Caleb edged his way closer to her, grateful for the warmth radiating from the old stove.

"Mornin'," he said.

"Good morning." She retrieved a covered plate from the sideboard and handed it to him. "You almost didn't make it in time. Martha brought only two pans of cinnamon rolls."

Her welcome sang through his heart like a hymn. "You saved this for me?"

She took his hat and hung it on the peg holding her coat. "I think half the town followed their noses in here this morning."

A sliver of hope worked into Caleb's chest as he pulled the checkered napkin from the plate. The spicy aroma made his mouth water, and he looked into her eyes.

"I kindly thank you, Annie."

She blushed and busied herself smoothing the creases from her apron. "You'll have to stand, I'm afraid, but it shouldn't be long. Milner, the editor, will no doubt be leaving soon since the paper comes out today."

Caleb remained at the group's edge, inhaling Martha Bobbins's handiwork and Whitaker's coffee. The men talked politics and claim jumpers, comparing both to an upcoming turkey shoot sponsored by Jedediah Cooper.

The saloon owner snagged a roll, waved it above his head and promised a twenty-dollar gold piece to the man who shot the biggest wild bird.

"More than a hundred men have already laid out the five-dollar entry fee," Cooper boasted. "But any of you could be the winner. Don't be left out."

"Not in here." Daniel Whitaker raised his voice above the cheers. "You'll not be doing your business in the mercantile. Take it elsewhere."

Cooper was ingenious, Caleb would give him that. But Whitaker was honorable.

Caleb glanced toward Annie and caught her pained expression. Something had happened between her and the saloon keeper, something unpleasant. Caleb felt the room's temperature spike.

God help Jedediah Cooper if he'd been inappropriate with Annie.

"Caleb?"

Her tone pulled him from morbid thoughts. She stared at his hand gripping the fork like a weapon.

He relaxed his fingers and cut another bite from the roll. Turning the other cheek was a worthy rule to follow, but not where a young woman was concerned. If Cooper offended Annie, Caleb would not be turning a cheek away from him, regardless of how ingenious the man appeared to be.

"Is something the matter?" She touched his arm as lightly as her voice touched his ear.

The gesture fired through him like heat roaring from Henry's forge. Sweat beaded at his hairline.

Martha called for Annie, and Caleb silently thanked the woman for her timely rescue. He stepped back as far as possible from the hot stove, afraid that he'd already filled the cramped room with stable perfume.

Chairs scooted across the floor, some snagging on the braided rug. Tin plates clattered in a dishpan on the stove, and Daniel Whitaker met his customers at the front counter, where he accepted their coins and thanks and wished them a good day. Martha busied herself with the dishes, and Annie ground coffee beans and filled the pot with fresh water.

Caleb pulled a low-back captain's chair away from the stove. His vengeful thoughts about Jedediah Cooper surprised him, but he stopped short of repentance. No man dared lay an unwanted hand on Annie Whitaker, and he didn't mind being the one to ensure that.

He didn't mind at all.

Because he was losing his heart to the spirited young woman, even though he'd sworn never to let such a thing happen again.

The brass bell sang out as the last customer left, and Daniel returned to the stove, where he chucked in a black lump from the coal bucket and adjusted the damper. He sat with a hefty sigh, rubbed his hands across his aproned girth and shook his head.

"Martha, you'll make a fat man of me yet."

Martha laughed and splashed at the sideboard, dunking plates in the rinsing pan and handing them to Annie, who dried them and stacked them on a shelf.

"Oh, Daniel, you are good for my heart."

Caleb glanced up from his disappearing breakfast and caught a boyish grin on the older man's face. He winked at Caleb and smoothed his mustache.

Caleb finished his cinnamon roll in three hearty bites. His plate had barely emptied when Annie's hand entered his view, open and waiting.

His first thought was to take her hand and kiss it, but he held himself in check. He had no idea how Annie would feel about such a gesture, and it wasn't his place to offer it. So he gave her a smile.

"Thank you, Annie."

She returned his smile, and her eyes lingered. Oh, Lord, how could he bear to see her every day, knowing he had nothing to give her but a broken heart and broken vows?

The bold truth sobered the warmth right out of him. He wrapped both hands around his cup, planted his elbows on his knees and stared at the braided rug beneath his feet. His eyes followed a red strand that wove through the pattern and circled halfway around the rug before giving way to a dark brown. Maybe he needed to give way himself, leave now rather than wait until spring. He could make Denver in three days. He'd saved enough to stake himself for a few weeks.

"You joining the hunt?" Daniel asked, breaking Caleb out of his reverie.

"No, sir. I don't own a rifle."

Daniel's mustache twitched and his eyes narrowed. "A cowboy like you with no gun?"

Too late Caleb recognized his blunder. "I have a side-arm, for snakes and such. But I've never been a hunter."

Whitaker leaned against his own knees, as much as his belly allowed. He threw a cautious look toward the women, who were still busy with the dishes, and then lowered his voice and looked Caleb dead in the eye.

"What *do* you do? And don't tell me you're good with horses. You're hiding something, son, and if you're taking an interest in my Annie—which I can see you are—you'd best be telling me now rather than later."

Chapter 10

Whitaker's stare burned like hot iron.

Caleb cleared his throat. He hadn't hidden his affections for Annie any better than he'd hidden himself from the Lord.

He huffed out a breath and decided to come clean. Annie and her father both deserved that, after all they'd done for him.

"I was a preacher."

The confession set Whitaker back in his chair, but he never took his eyes off Caleb. One white brow cocked like a pistol hammer. "That explains it."

Exposed, Caleb started to rise. Whitaker stopped him with a quick hand.

"You've got a way with words. I heard it when you prayed over breakfast that day, and I hear it when you talk to Annie." He looked up as the women went into the back room. Then he asked, "What happened?"

Caleb breathed easier with Annie and Martha out of earshot. He thought of the old man in his dream, who looked nothing like Daniel Whitaker, but maybe there was a connection.

Maybe confession was a stop on the journey home.

"I pastored a small church back in Saint Joseph, on the edge of town. About forty people." He paused for a moment, adjusting to the sensation of talking about himself for the first time in a long time. "I wasn't any good. No converts. Just the same people every Sunday, living the same lives." He cut a look toward Whitaker. "Except one."

Might as well spill it all.

"She wasn't living the life I thought she was. Then she accepted a wealthy banker's proposal—a man who also happened to be on the deacon board."

Whitaker reached for the coal bucket and added another piece to the stove. "Over yours."

Caleb nodded, feeling the fool again.

"So you left."

Whitaker's look was more compassionate than judgmental, but Caleb didn't want the man's pity. He wanted the man's daughter, and that was becoming more unlikely by the minute.

"I figured those people needed a real pastor. Someone older with more experience. I sent word to the seminary so they could find someone else."

Whitaker leaned back in his chair. "So who called you to preach?"

There it was—the question Caleb had dodged for half a year until recently. He knew the answer, he just didn't know why his calling hadn't worked out.

He met Whitaker's eyes and caught Annie's fire in them.

"God called me."

"And do you suppose God changes His mind about that sort of thing?"

Seminary lectures scrolled through his memory, but Whitaker's question made it personal. "No, sir."

"You're familiar with the eighth chapter of Romans, the twenty-eighth verse?"

He was. It lay like a banked ember awaiting discovery. "We know that all things work together for good to them that love God, to them who are the called according to His purpose."

The called.

The words scorched Caleb's soul.

"You can't outrun God, son. I'm no preacher, but I for sure know that much."

Annie came in from the back room, and the flame in Caleb's chest burned deeper. Her eyes lit on his, and her smile nearly sucked the breath from his lungs. What would she think if she knew the truth?

He shoved his hat on. Or rather, *when* she knew the truth.

He needed distance. Perspective. Air.

He stood and set his cup in the dishpan. "Thank you, ladies." He turned to Whitaker. "And you, sir." Then he left the store before he crumbled to ash in front of them.

Cold air slapped his face and bit through his shirt as he made his way back to the livery. He shoved through the door and into a wall of heat. Fire blazed in Henry's brick furnace. Everywhere—extremes.

Caleb grabbed the pitchfork as he walked up the alleyway. "Mornin'."

Henry's hammer paused in its dance against the anvil, and he looked at Caleb. "And a good one it is."

For some.

"After I finish the stalls, I'll be heading out for a while. Be in this evening."

Henry took a step back and craned his neck toward the spare harnesses and tack hanging against the last stall.

"Everything is mended and soaped," Caleb said. "Finished Saturday night. The Turk brothers and Hancock are already gone."

Henry took to his work. No frown, no affirmation. "Fine by me."

Caleb reached for the wheelbarrow and pushed it into the alleyway. He could never tell what Henry was thinking unless the man came right out and said it plain.

Caleb should take lessons.

Nell whiffled a low greeting as he opened her gate. "Missing Annie, are you?" The mare tossed her head as if she understood and rumbled deep in her chest.

I know the feeling.

By noon he had the stalls cleaned and fresh bedding laid for all fifteen horses and mules inside. He saddled Rooster and hand-fed Sally a fistful of oats. "Maybe next time, ol' girl." He rubbed the bay mare's shoulder, truly hoping for a next time. "If the way is easy and Annie doesn't change her mind, we just might be taking another ride before the big snows fly."

Or he might be riding on out of town alone, snow or not. He hoped to have some direction after his trek today.

He buttoned his waistcoat and duster against the cold, then mounted the gelding and rode through town, half expecting Annie to be sweeping the boardwalk in front of the mercantile. As he passed by, he saw her busy inside with a customer. Just as well.

The river ran low and easy enough to cross, but he kept to the north side and Rooster took quick to the trail. Slate-blue clouds hunched over the distant ridges, threatening a storm. A soaking might be part and parcel of his day.

He needed a good drenching, something to wash away his indecision and wring out the uncertainty in his soul.

He skirted the brick-colored granite guarding the canyon across from the Indian encampment. Mountain Utes, he'd been told. Wintering near the mineral springs, living off deer that fed along the river.

Beyond the red monolith, the canyon tightened to a narrow green valley that hugged the river with cottonwood clusters, bushy grass and spiny, fingerlike cacti. A wide creek spilled from cedar-scattered hills on the south side and joined the river in laughter.

A merry heart doeth good like a medicine. He'd give all his earnings for a merry heart, or at least the understanding of what was weighing him down.

The dream had unsettled him, and it hung with him still. Especially after today's inquisition by Daniel Whitaker. He didn't begrudge the man's watchful eye for his daughter, but he'd cut near to the quick.

It didn't take a seer to know what the dream meant. It was about a kind of homecoming. Trouble was, Caleb didn't know where home was because he didn't have one. Hadn't had one since he'd left his parents' place for school and the ministry.

The farther he rode, the more carefully Rooster chose his footing on the roughening trail. An occasional piñon pushed up through the rocky soil, holding its own in the rugged landscape. The hills pulled themselves into straight-walled battlements, red rock layers jutting out like planks at a sawmill. Scrub oak and juniper jammed the rock crevices.

An unforgiving land, it seemed.

Perfect for an unforgiving heart.

Was that it? Had he not forgiven Mollie and the deacon? Himself? God?

The canyon suddenly narrowed. Granite walls rose

hundreds of feet in shades of pink and gray and ocher, and beside him the river raised its voice, complaining loudly where boulders blocked its path.

Just like him.

His complaints were silent, but they were complaints nonetheless, shouting in his soul, drowning out his meager gratitude.

He startled at a sudden movement and yanked Rooster to a stop. Had the four deer not been leaping up the barren rock face, he would not have seen them—a family of three does and a young buck. Stunned, he watched them climb the tawny granite on unseen footholds, bounding up to the treeless rim rock and out of sight.

Effortlessly.

He maketh my feet like hinds' feet, and setteth me upon my high places.

Those live coals kept falling into his mind, like a glowing, burning rockslide. Everywhere he looked, he saw scripture played out before him. Had the Lord hobbled him in one spot so all he could see was what God wanted him to see?

The realization struck him like a blow. He'd always believed those lofty places to be forested hilltops, lush with knee-high grass and gentle streams. He looked up again at the forbidding rock wall, almost doubting he'd seen the deer scale its face and leap to the top.

Almost.

"*He* makes my feet like hinds' feet." Rooster swiveled his ears at Caleb's voice, pulled at the reins and reached for a grassy cluster struggling through the smooth river rocks. "It's Your work, isn't it?"

He laughed at his sudden clarity. It was all God's work—the hearts of his former parishioners, his calling, his climb through imposing circumstances. All he had to do was sur-render. Come home.

His eyes stung, and the rushing river blurred before him as he pulled Rooster around and headed downstream.

A shadow dimmed the sun, and he looked behind him to a roiling gray cloud hanging over the canyon walls. A feathery flake settled on his hand, another on his leg. A sudden gust funneling through the canyon tugged at his hat. He screwed it down tighter and touched his heels to Rooster's side, urging him along the rocky path.

By the time he made the cottonwood clearing, snow had dusted the trees and grass in a sugar-fine powder. At the town's edge, Caleb quickened Rooster to a lope. He dismounted at the livery and led the horse into the stable to unsaddle.

Sally sheltered beneath the livery's long eaves as Caleb ran Rooster into the corral. The gelding joined his trail partner and together they stood slack-eared, rumps against the building, watching the snow. Silence blanketed the town, the stock pens. All lay still beneath the settling white.

Grateful for his accommodations, Caleb went inside.

He'd spend the next few days listening. Not complaining, not licking his wounds—listening. Looking to the wounds of his Lord and listening for His voice.

Annie rolled the pin across the floured dough, cut eight large biscuits with a baking powder can and laid them in a greased skillet. Gathering the leftover dough to roll again, she looked for the third time over her shoulder at the front door.

Where was he?

Caleb hadn't been back for breakfast since the morning Martha Bobbins had brought cinnamon rolls, and that was nearly two weeks ago. Was he waiting for more of the same? Were Annie's "potbellied" biscuits no longer good enough?

Had he been toying with her when he mentioned taking her to ride up the river?

Had he left town?

Tears pooled against her lashes, and she swiped the drops away with a floured hand. She'd been too busy to visit Nell—and thus see about Caleb. It seemed there were always several customers in the store at once, laying up for the coming holidays. And by the time her father closed each evening, it was dark and cold and she couldn't bring herself to make the trip to the livery alone.

She recalled the Sunday stroll near Martha's home, that gloriously golden day that left her thinking more frequently of Caleb, reminding her that there was so very much she didn't know about him.

Edna would say Annie had lost her grip falling for a man of no means. What future could she possibly have with someone she knew so little about? But, oh, the gentleness with which he'd tended her thorn-pricked finger and tucked her hand inside his arm.

A tear escaped and spotted the flour-dusted sideboard. Again she swiped her face, irritated that a man would make her cry. Despite her resolve, she stomped her left foot hard against the floorboards.

The brass bell sang and hope flashed only to fade at the sound of Martha's lilting voice.

"Good morning, dears." Martha pushed her bonnet back and bustled to the stove, where Annie's father prodded coal chunks with a long poker, settling them just so on last night's banked coals. She laid a hand against his bent shoulder and a kiss upon his cheek. The blood rushed to his face, and he glanced at Annie as if caught committing the unspeakable.

Annie turned away to stifle yet another onslaught of tears bent on escape.

She'd soon be the only unwed Whitaker in her family. Edna's last letter had announced her engagement to Jonathan Mitchell, just as Annie had expected. And she also expected that her father and Martha would be announcing a similar pledge. Some things were simply too clear to ignore.

"Annie, your coffee smells delicious. Might I have a cup?"

Before she could answer, her father snatched a mug from the sideboard, filled it with the hot brew and scooped sugar from a covered bowl. He handed the cup to Martha with smitten adoration.

Annie pounded the extra dough and squeezed it through her fists. She would not cry. Why shouldn't her father show such affection for the seamstress? Martha had brightened his life in a way that Annie and her sister had never been able to, even though he loved them dearly. And Annie had wanted this for him since the moment she'd first realized Martha had feelings for him. She should be happy for her father.

"Where is your young man?"

Martha's unexpected question sent a stinging dart through Annie's chest. She blinked hard, mashed the final biscuits into the skillet and carried it to the stove. *Her* young man? Hardly. For all she knew he had settled into a fancy Denver hotel, or found work on another cattle spread between here and there.

Or been robbed and murdered.

She sucked in a breath at the wicked thought and caught Martha's questioning gaze.

"Are you all right, dear?"

"Quite." Annie's spine stiffened. "I have no young man.

But if you might be referring to Mr. Hutton, I've no idea where he is."

"Oh, my." Martha's sweet face sobered. "I'm so sorry to have upset you."

Annie's chin raised involuntarily. "I'm not upset." The sharp edge to her voice forced her to face Martha and offer an explanation. Taking the chair next to the kindhearted woman, she folded her apron around her hands to hide her agitation.

"He hasn't been back since the day you brought your wonderful cinnamon rolls."

Martha's emotions warred visibly—pleasure over Annie's compliment and regret over the news. She looked to Daniel. "Do you think he's left?"

Annie's father stroked his mustache, dipped his brows and looked everywhere except at Annie.

Did he know something she did not?

She sat straighter and held him with an unwavering glare.

"I imagine he's just been busy at the livery." Daniel raised his cup to his lips, looking straight at Annie above the rim as if giving her a secret message.

Annie didn't need to be told twice.

She jumped to her feet and hurried into their private quarters, where she yanked the star quilt from her bed and rolled it into a tight bundle. Surely he needed one in that drafty old barn. Then she grabbed her scarf and mittens, pulled on her woolen cloak and paused by the stove.

"Martha, do you mind watching the biscuits for me? I have an errand that I must run immediately before business picks up and I can't get away."

Martha's eyes darted from Annie to her father, and a rosy tint warmed her cheeks. "I would be happy to, dear.

Take your time. Daniel and I can handle everything." She reached over and patted his arm. "Isn't that so?"

Annie's father coughed and shifted in his chair. "Of course we can." Then he stood and followed Annie to the door.

"Be careful, Annie girl." He patted the quilt and leaned nearer. "And listen with your heart."

She had half a mind to ask him exactly what it was that he knew, but she didn't. All she said was "I will, Daddy."

And then she bolted out the door.

The boardwalk rang beneath her heels as she strode toward the livery. What if Caleb wasn't there? What if he really had left?

And what would people think of her carrying a quilt to the stable?

She glanced about at the few people out so early, all men. Those who caught her eye nodded or touched their hat brims in a respectful greeting. Most were businessmen on their way to work. A few were miners down from the camps for the winter. But since when did she care what others thought?

Squeezing the bundle against her waist, she hurried on.

The boardwalk ended at the bank building, and she hiked her skirt as she stepped down to the dirt. No dust blew in the street today, just the dry cold that was so unlike Omaha's damp winters. Her breath advanced ahead in a cloudy puff.

Five horses occupied the corral at the livery, their breath rising white from soft muzzles to vanish above their ears. She slowed her steps as she approached the wide doors opened only inches. Delivering a quilt had seemed like the perfect excuse back in the mercantile. Now she wasn't so sure. What would she say?

She stopped and tugged her scarf higher against her

chin. Then gripping one door's edge, she pulled it open and slipped into the stable.

A smoky tang struck her lungs, and for a moment fear clutched her heart. But the steady *ping, ping, ping* of metal on metal reminded her that Henry's blacksmith shop filled the back of the stable. As her eyes adjusted to the dim interior, she saw him at the anvil with his back to her, just beyond the last stall. Her shoulders relaxed, and she faced the box stall where she and her father had once lived.

The door was swung wide, and she stopped on the threshold. A black-and-white cat curled tightly on a bedroll lying atop a thick straw layer. A Bible lay nearby. In the near corner stood an upturned crate with a basin, pitcher and oil lamp, and on one wall hung a saddle, blankets and bridle.

It might all be Caleb's. Nothing betrayed its owner, though she remembered the plain white pitcher and basin he had bought from the mercantile. But if he'd left, he'd leave those behind.

Her heart sank. No hat or coat lay about that she recognized. Her gaze lit on the Bible. Did he have one?

"Looking for someone?"

The deep voice sent her off balance, and she stumbled forward into the stall. A strong hand caught her arm and steadied her, and she turned to see a bearded man with dark, laughing eyes.

Gathering her wits and clinging madly to the quilt, Annie took a deep breath. "Caleb."

One corner of his mouth twitched. "You were looking for someone else?"

"No! I mean— No."

What would Edna do in this situation?

Annie pulled her overly warm scarf away from her throat. Never mind Edna.

"Where have you been?"

His sudden grin made her wish she'd not been so bold. He leaned against the doorframe and folded his arms across his chest. A two-week growth hugged his jawline and gave him a rugged, almost dangerous look. "You were worried?"

Frustrated by his teasing, she raised her chin and thrust the rolled quilt at him.

"Here. Maybe you can use this."

Caleb caught the bundle before it fell and his expression shifted to surprise. "Thank you."

She stepped forward as if to pass, but he remained in the doorway.

"Excuse me, but I came to check on Nell." Annie held her ground, inches from him, close enough to feel his warmth.

His gaze traveled to her lips before returning to her eyes, and his breath dusted her face.

What would she do if he kissed her?

What would she do if he didn't?

"Thank you," he repeated softly. He leaned closer.

She held her breath.

"Nell is doing just fine."

Heat flooded Annie's cheeks, and she hurried past, gratefully turning her back on Caleb as she made for the mare's stall. A soft nicker greeted her, and she regretted having no treat for the mother-to-be. She'd left the mercantile in such a hurry that she hadn't thought to bring dried apples or a few carrots.

Annie held her cheek against the mare's warm head and stroked her thick neck. "You poor dear. Just look at you."

The horse's belly hung like a bulging grain sack, distended and heavy with promise. Yet for all her size and distortion, Nell seemed calm and unconcerned.

Footsteps sounded behind Annie, and she sensed Caleb's closeness.

"I owe you an explanation," he said, his voice low and rough as ground coffee.

He moved closer, leaned over the stall gate and combed his fingers through Nell's mane.

Annie's pulse quickened as she remembered her father's words: *Listen with your heart.*

She swallowed. Listening with your heart meant opening your heart.

Was she ready to open her heart to Caleb Hutton?

Or had she already done so without realizing it?

Chapter 11

Lilacs bloomed in winter with Annie so close that Caleb could bury his face in her hair. The impulse nearly overwhelmed him, but he forced his mind to focus on what he had to say rather than what he yearned to do.

"I'm not who you think I am."

She looked at him, doubt and expectation in her eyes. "And who do I think you are, other than what you've led me to believe?"

She wasn't going to make it easy, but then she wouldn't be Annie if she did.

"I left out some things." He uttered a silent prayer before he said, "I'm a preacher. Or at least I was."

Annie gasped. Her eyes rounded, and she turned to the mare.

He leaned against the stall gate. Nell flicked her tail and craned over the railing toward Annie's coat pocket.

"No apples today, girl." Annie's gentle tone shot hope

through his chest. Perhaps she'd show him the same consideration, though he didn't deserve it.

Annie kept her eyes on the mare as she stroked the broad head. "Why did you say you were good with horses, a ranch hand?"

A fair question. He propped his right arm across the gate top and angled himself to see her reaction. "Remember when Abraham told Pharaoh that Sarah was his sister?"

Annie's fine brow creased at the bridge of her nose.

"It was true," he said. "Sarah *was* Abraham's sister. But it was only half the truth."

"So you're saying that you told my father and me only half the truth."

"Yes."

"Why?"

He cleared his throat and pushed away from the stall door to face her squarely. No more hedging. He'd run from a broken heart and broken a vow in the process. If he wasn't man enough to tell Annie Whitaker the whole truth, face-to-face, then he wasn't man enough for anything.

"My father was a veterinarian. He wanted me to follow in his profession, taught me much of it as I was growing up." He rubbed the back of his neck. "But I believed, at the time, that I was called to preach the Gospel. My father conceded and helped pay my way through seminary."

She looked at him as if mining for the truth. "So you really *do* have a way with horses."

He allowed himself to give her a brief smile, but pressed on. "My first and only church was in Saint Joseph, Missouri. A small congregation. No new converts, but good people. Faithful. Except for one." He stopped to gauge Annie's reaction, but he couldn't tell what she was thinking. "I gave my heart to a girl who chose a wealthy deacon instead. Rather than stay and face them from the pulpit, I convinced myself that the people needed an older pastor, one with more experience and wisdom."

He paused, dread curdling in his stomach.

"I left. Turned my back on God and preaching and headed west to cowboy on the Lazy R."

With this final confession, the tension in his neck and shoulders eased.

Annie had removed her mittens and loosened the scarf from her throat, and she threaded its fringe in and out between her fingers. Her eyes met his with no sign of scorn or derision. "And like Jonah, you ended up where you didn't want to be."

He heaved out a breath at her comparison, grateful she hadn't called him a coward and stomped out of the barn.

"Why didn't you go home to your father?"

"My parents are no longer living. The next best thing was a ranch out west."

Annie reached for the dozing mare's forelock. "Do you still plan to leave here, too? Come spring, like you said earlier?"

Not if you give me reason to stay.

But he couldn't tell her that. Not now, not yet. What did he have to offer? Life as a laborer's wife?

"I'll look for another church and start over. Maybe take up a circuit and preach in the gold camps."

"I saw the Bible on your bedroll," she said. "Have you made your peace with God?"

He hooked his thumbs in his waistcoat. "You make it sound like I'm about to bite the dust."

She laughed, and the sound warmed his insides. The dread he'd felt anticipating her response began to melt away.

"In a way you already have," she said. "You've died to yourself if you're brave enough to try again."

He would not call himself *brave,* but the clear sense of

her words breathed hope into him, fanning the belief that God had forgiven him and offered him a second chance.

Would she?

Annie pulled her mittens on and stepped back from the stall.

"You haven't answered my question about where you've been the last two weeks. We've missed you at breakfast." A slight blush tinted her cheeks as she moved toward the barn doors.

"I had to 'make my peace with God,' as you put it. Clear my head, get things straight."

"And you couldn't do that at the mercantile?"

Dare he tell her he could think of nothing but her when he was at the mercantile?

Silhouetted in the open stable door, she stopped and spoke over her shoulder. "I was afraid you didn't like my potbellied biscuits anymore."

Her teasing tone cleared the air. He shook his head and held one hand against his stomach. "I've sorely missed them. But I'll be back if you'll have me."

And then she faced him with luminous eyes. "And why wouldn't I? You promised me a ride up the river."

All the breath left his lungs as she turned and walked out the door. He leaned back against the railing and scrubbed his hands over his face and thickening beard. And then he remembered her gift.

He walked into what he'd come to think of as his room and lifted the rolled quilt. He buried his face in a bright star, inhaling Annie's scent.

Thank You, Lord.

The cat rubbed against his leg and offered her sleepy opinion.

"There's hope," he said, kneeling to run his hand along her back. "Today I've been given hope."

He'd take Annie on that ride the next chance he got—if it didn't snow. He didn't want to wait for spring, because come spring, he'd be riding out on his own. The prospect pulled his heart in the opposite direction, but he'd known for several days that he was to return to the ministry. It was the right thing to do. Would Annie wait for him if he rode a mining camp circuit? Or join him if he found another church far from Cañon City? Would her father let her?

He laid the quilt on his bedroll and walked down the alleyway to where he'd earlier left his duster and hat on a nail. The print shop had paper. He'd write to his seminary, see if the gold camps or larger towns farther north needed a preacher.

She *knew* it.

Only she hadn't.

Annie hugged her cloak tighter. Caleb Hutton *had* been hiding something all right, but she hadn't pegged him as a preacher. Her fingers tingled in her mittens—not from the cold weather but from excitement.

Excitement? Over the fact that Caleb was a preacher?

No, that wasn't it. But what?

She tucked her hands beneath her arms and slowed her pace.

He didn't seem like a preacher. But what should a preacher look like, act like? Quiet, intelligent, gentle. She laughed aloud. Her pastoral characterization fit Nell better than Reverend Hartman. He was intelligent and gentle, but she'd never classify him as quiet. The man exuded energy, joked with his small congregation and flirted unashamedly with Hannah Baker, his bride-to-be.

Come to think of it, Annie's pastor from back home met all three qualities, but he was, well, *boring.* Caleb Hutton was anything but boring.

She opened the mercantile door to welcoming warmth. Her father and Martha sat by the stove chatting while Karl Turk picked through a notions box on the counter.

Did her father even know the man was in the store?

"Can I help you, Mr. Turk?" Annie stuffed her mittens and scarf behind the counter, laid her wrap over a crate and scowled at her father. Either he was going deaf or he was so helplessly smitten with Martha Bobbins that he had ears for no one but the seamstress.

Turk grumbled and poked through the box.

"Are you looking for something in particular?" Annie's voice raised on the last word and she tied on an apron as she watched the lumberman's thick fingers fail to catch on any item.

"A razor," he said. "But I can't find one in all these gew-gaws and baubles."

"Oh, the *razors* are over here." She turned to the shelf behind her and threw one last glance at her father. He caught it and erupted from his chair as if burned by spilt coffee.

Red-faced he hurried to Annie's side. "Razors, you say. I got a fine assortment in on the last shipment." He winked at Annie and pulled a long box from the shelf.

She frowned as if scolding a spoiled child, but there was no use staying mad at her jovial parent. It was impossible. Besides, her own spirits were so light she fairly skimmed across the rough floorboards. She gathered her cloak, scarf and mittens and headed toward Martha, who was washing her cup in the dishpan.

"You don't need to wash your dishes here," Annie said.

"Oh, yes, I do." Martha clicked her tongue and shook her head. "If Daniel hadn't been so caught up in our conversation, he would have known Mr. Turk was here." She dried the cup, set it aside and pushed a few stray hairs beneath her cap. Looking at Annie like a shy schoolgirl, she blushed. "I didn't even hear the bell myself."

Annie laughed and hugged the little woman's rounded shoulders. "Never you mind. It all worked out." She poured herself some coffee and added sugar from a covered bowl. "I think he's quite taken with you, Martha."

The seamstress blushed even more and pulled at an invisible thread on her skirt. "Do you mind, dear?"

"No, I do not." She smiled at the older woman's nervousness. "I think it's wonderful. My father has been alone far too long—even with me and my sister."

As she uttered the words, her heart trembled at the thought of living by herself in the storeroom, but she forced the worry away.

Martha held her in a knowing gaze. "Did you find your young man?"

Annie allowed a smile to pull at her lips. "Yes, I did. And I gave him the quilt." Dare she share her secret with Martha, tell her that she was losing her heart to a wayward preacher-turned-cowboy?

"I really must be going." Martha lifted her wrap from a chair and snugged it around her shoulders.

Annie followed her to the door in time to hear Mr. Turk mention Christmas trees.

"I brought several down from my last trip to the Greenhorns," he said. "They're out behind my place by the river. If you don't mind spreadin' the word, I'm sellin' 'em for two bits a piece."

How splendid to have a tree for Christmas, festooned in popcorn garland and round, red cranberries. Well, maybe black chokecherries out here in the Rocky Mountains.

"I'll take one, Mr. Turk," Martha said. Turning to Annie's father, she softened her voice. "Could you drive my buckboard down and pick it up for me?"

"I'd love to have one for the store window, too," Annie said, watching her father calculating the tree's cost against the opportunity to visit his sweetheart. She turned to Martha. "Will two trees fit on your wagon?"

"I believe they would." Martha dug a coin from her reticule and handed it to Mr. Turk. "Twenty-five cents, paid in advance."

He smiled and tipped his hat. "Thank you, ma'am. I'll set one out as soon as I get home."

"Well?" Annie eyed her father and caught the glint in his eye as he dug in his pocket for a coin.

"Make that two trees, Turk. I'll be by after I walk Miss Bobbins home and stop at the livery for her buckboard."

Annie almost envied her father. She hadn't ridden in a buggy or even a buckboard since their arrival in town. And she had so wanted to visit the great canyon upriver with Caleb. Would he act on the bold statement she'd made at the livery?

"I'll mind the store while you're gone, but don't dally." She gave her father a playful pat on his shoulder as he shrugged into his coat.

"I managed to get the mail out, so that's one less worry for you. I'll be back shortly."

That wasn't likely, but she'd not begrudge him a change of pace after the daylight-to-dark hours he put in.

As soon as he stepped through the door and closed it behind him, Martha tucked her hand in his arm and they headed up the boardwalk. Annie checked the fire and set about clearing the window display to make room for the tree.

She removed dry goods from the heavy oak table and set them on the counter. As she leaned into the table to shove it against the far wall, a shadow lingered at the window, and she looked up to see Jedediah Cooper hovering like a hawk ready to sweep down on its prey.

Her blood chilled.

He moved to the door before she could lock it; the bell tolled as he stepped inside. Instinctively she hurried behind the counter and reached for the broom.

"I was afraid the mercantile was closed when I saw your father stepping out with the widow Bobbins." Cooper's voice slid around the words like snake oil as he closed the door and loosened the muffler from his neck.

Annie's fingers tightened on the broom handle and she raised her chin, determined to not show fear. "How can I help you, Mr. Cooper?"

His lips curled in a sly smile, and he raked a hungry leer across her body. "Don't be so formal, Annie. By all means, call me Jed." With great aplomb he pulled the gloves from his hands one finger at a time. "You may *help* me, Annie, by considering an update of our arrangement for your occupation of the back portion of this fine establishment."

Annie breathed slowly through her nose, hoping to prevent red anger from surging into her face. "We already reached an agreement, Mr. Cooper. You *agreed* to our offer before my father and I moved in six weeks ago."

Cooper laid his gloves on the counter and slowly made his way to the end, where he breached Annie's sanctuary. She backed toward the opposite end, never taking her eyes from Cooper, mentally measuring how far she was from escape.

"All agreements are subject to change. Didn't I mention that?"

He lunged for her. She swung the broom at his face, but he fended it off, sending it over the counter.

Annie bolted for the door. Her fingers gripped the knob and turned. He grabbed her from behind, one arm around her waist, a hand over her mouth. He whirled her around. As her hand slipped off the knob, the door swung open, clanging the bell.

"Not so fast," he breathed against her neck. Stale tobacco from his coat sleeve vied with his whiskey-laced breath, and her stomach lurched. "We're meant to be, Annie. I knew it when you fell into my arms. So soft and warm." He spread his fingers to crush her nose, as well. She kicked at his legs and dug her fingers into his smothering hand.

Was that what he intended? To cut off her air until she passed out and then—

His throaty laugh twisted through her. "You're a fighter. That's good. I like my women a little feisty."

She reached up, groping for his face. He swore and hefted her like a sack of flour past the counter, past the chairs, the stove.

Oh, God, help me. She clawed at his fingers. Her lungs screamed for air and her vision blurred, darkening at the edges.

She had to keep fighting.

Squeezed against him, she felt the growl deep in his chest before she heard it. Then he pushed through the curtain and into the darkened back room.

Chapter 12

Caleb thanked Milner, the *Cañon City Times* editor, whom he left sifting through notes on a cluttered corner desk. He tucked a folded newspaper and extra notepaper into his waistcoat and exited the print shop.

His glance immediately went to the mercantile. Before he'd stepped into the print shop, he'd seen Daniel and Martha walking down the boardwalk. He'd also seen Jedediah Cooper standing in front of Whitaker's. The dandy had pulled at his cuffs, looked both ways along the street and walked into the store.

Maybe he should pay a visit to the mercantile himself. He didn't want that man anywhere near Annie, landlord or no. He rubbed his left elbow and jabbed a finger through the thinning material. He could use a new shirt. Might as well get one now.

He adjusted his hat and stepped off the boardwalk. As he approached the mercantile, he saw that the door was wide open, which was strange, given how cold it was outside.

His neck prickled as if lightning were about to strike, and before he even understood why, Caleb broke into a run.

Without looking both ways, he flew into the path of an oncoming buckboard. The horse reared, and the driver pulled up and hollered. Caleb reached for the startled animal's bridle and spoke soothingly as he rubbed the horse's neck and withers.

"Sorry about that," he said to the driver.

"Watch where you're going!"

Caleb stepped back and tipped his hat as the angry farmer drove by.

He checked the street and ran across to the opposite boardwalk.

When he reached the mercantile's open door, he thought of his Colt revolver tucked beneath his bedroll.

No time for that now.

He stepped inside and saw Annie's broom on the floor. No one sat at the stove. His heart galloped into his throat.

He softened his steps and crossed the wooden floor as if approaching a wounded animal. A scuffling behind the curtain convinced Caleb that Annie was in harm's way, and that he would be wounding whatever animal he found there—man or beast.

His fingers curled into fists, and he held his breath.

In his heart, Caleb knew Annie would not invite a man into her sleeping quarters, especially with her father gone. Yet still, a flash of Mollie Sullivan on her beau's arm stabbed at Caleb's memory. He clenched his jaw, reminding himself that Annie was not Mollie, and pushed through the curtain.

Like a giant slug, Cooper's body pinned Annie to her cot. One hand held her wrists above her head, the other pressed against her mouth. Fear screamed from her eyes, louder than Caleb's hammering heart.

He'd never wanted to kill another human being. Until now.

Cooper must have seen Annie's eyes lock on Caleb, for the man glanced over his shoulder. Caleb jerked him to his feet, spun him around and smashed his fist into Cooper's sputtering explanation. Blood spurted from the man's nose and a dark gash opened above his lip.

He dropped to the floor, out cold.

Stunned and breathing hard, Annie pushed up on her elbows, her eyes dark pools in her ashen face. Caleb's chest heaved with murderous emotion as he opened and closed his fists and struggled to gather his wits.

He held Annie's eyes with his own until she flung herself into his arms, sobbing and trembling. Encircling her, he forced his thoughts from the man on the floor to the woman weeping against him. Her beautiful hair tumbled down her back, and he buried both hands in it, pressing her to his chest.

He pulled his voice from a place deep inside and willed it into softness.

"Did he hurt you?"

Annie shook her head from side to side beneath his hand, and he felt her broken sobs as she fought for control.

"No," she whispered. "But if you hadn't come—"

His eyes burned, and bile rose in his throat.

With a steadying breath, Annie relaxed in his embrace and looked into his eyes. "I prayed. I cried out for God to help me."

Tears welled anew and spilled into rivulets down her reddened cheeks. He thumbed them away and smoothed her unruly hair from her face.

"I never dreamed it would be you who rescued me." A sudden breath convulsed in her chest, and she shuddered. "How did you know?"

Hesitant to let her go, he released one arm and guided

her through the curtain to the chairs at the stove. Settling her into the closest one, he squeezed her fingers before releasing them completely. "Give me a minute."

He cut two lengths of twine at the counter, tied the curtain back with the shorter one to keep an eye on Cooper and bound the man's hands in several loops with the other. Then he pulled a chair close to Annie and reached again for her hands.

"I was at the printing office. On my way in, I saw Cooper walk in here. When I came out just a minute or two later, I noticed the door was open, and something didn't seem right to me."

She clutched his hands like a drowning woman grasping a rope. "Daddy will never forgive himself for leaving me alone. It could spoil everything for him."

Puzzled, Caleb studied her face. "What do you mean, Annie?"

"Daddy and Martha," she said. Letting out a deep sigh, she pulled her hands away and twisted her hair into a knot at her neck. "I fully expect them to—" She looked away. "They haven't yet made a declaration, but Mr. Cooper said…"

Her voice trailed off as she held her hair with one hand, searching through the folds of her skirt with the other.

Her combs.

He stepped over Cooper's unconscious hulk and rage churned again. He retrieved the combs from Annie's cot, where they'd worked loose, and pressed them into her hand.

"Thank you. Again."

He might as well be the one drowning—he kept getting lost in her beautiful eyes, which were full of tears.

"Cooper said what?"

She didn't seem ready to say. Caleb wrestled with a question he had to ask, *needed* to ask. Annie's earlier discomfort at the mention of Cooper had hinted at trouble. He shoved his fervor down and calmed his voice.

"Annie, I have to ask you—has Cooper ever tried anything like this before today?"

Her face blanched, but she shook her head.

"The day I asked him about renting the storeroom, I was pushed into his arms."

Caleb said nothing, waiting for more.

"I went to the saloon to talk to him, but I went no farther than just inside the door. As I stood there, someone outside pushed the door from behind. I lost my balance and fell against him."

She glanced at Cooper's still form and shuddered.

"Did he hurt you then?" Revenge skirted Caleb's thoughts, goading him to finish what he'd started with the scoundrel.

She shook her head again. "No. But I was humiliated. The way he looked at me—"

Again he encased her hand in his. "He'll not try it again, I promise you. You were going to tell me something, something he said. What was it?"

Fresh tears formed against her lashes, and she wiped them away. "Today he said if I told Daddy, he'd kick us out of the mercantile."

Caleb pulled air in through his nose as hate filled him. God help him, he wanted to do a lot more than just hate Jedediah Cooper.

"That won't happen. I'll be speaking with the magistrate as soon as your father returns, and I intend to tell him the whole story."

"I'm so ashamed." The chin that usually took every assault from a lofty perch drooped against her chest.

"No, Annie." Gently, he tilted her face to meet his eyes. "You have nothing to be ashamed of. Nothing at all."

He longed to tell her how he felt, but now wasn't the time. She was too vulnerable. He'd wait.

Heavy footsteps fell across the threshold, and Daniel Whitaker's voice boomed into the store. "Did you see me coming with this monstrosity and leave the door open?"

Whitaker held the cut end of a large evergreen as he dragged it through the door. Both Caleb and Annie rose to help him.

One look at Annie's disheveled appearance and Daniel dropped the tree and reached for his daughter.

"Caleb Hutton!" he thundered.

"Daddy, it's not what you think." Annie threw her arms around her father's waist. "He saved me, Daddy. He came just in time."

A moan from the back room drew their attention to the man on the floor. Caleb bolted to Cooper and hefted him to his feet. Blood stained Cooper's shirtfront and brocade vest, and he held his bound hands to his broken nose.

Caleb grabbed his arm and shoved him past the stove toward the store's front. "Tell Whitaker what happened, Cooper, or I will."

Red-faced and sputtering, the man's eyes darted between Annie, her father and escape. Caleb stepped around him and soundly shut the door.

Annie stood with her arm linked through her father's as they watched Caleb usher Jedediah Cooper, none too gently, to the magistrate's office.

"Annie, girl, I never would have forgiven myself if that man had hurt you."

She hugged his arm and looked into his guilt-reddened eyes. "I shouldn't have gone to the saloon, Daddy. I should have listened to you. You were right."

He pulled her into a fatherly embrace and cupped her

head in his big hand. "I've been thinking too much about myself lately and not enough about you."

Annie pulled away to look him in the eyes. "Nonsense, Daddy. You've been happy, and that has made me happy."

Her father blushed and blustered and pulled Annie into a hug. "I'm just glad you're all right."

"Have you delivered Martha's tree yet?"

"Don't know that I'll ever view a Christmas tree the same after today."

Still shaken from the ordeal, she willed her nerves to calm and steadied her voice. Brushing aside her father's comment, she reached for the aromatic tree that lay across their floor. "I'm not letting Jedediah Cooper spoil my Christmas and neither should you."

If she quaked at every horrible thing that *might* have happened, she'd cower herself into an early grave.

She closed her eyes and pressed her face into the branches. "This smells so good. Help me set it in the window."

"Let's lean it against the wall. Turk showed me how to make a cross and nail it to the tree bottom so it'll stand by itself. I've got an old box out back that I can bust up and use. Be right back."

Her father stopped suddenly and pegged her with a warning. "You holler if anyone comes in, and I'll be here in a flash."

Her heart warmed at his protective nature, and she resisted the urge to follow him outside. "I'll be fine, Daddy. Besides, I can just topple this blue spruce on anyone who is less than gentlemanly."

He wagged his head as he headed for the back.

Annie's thoughts wandered to her other protector. A shiver coursed through her body as she recalled the chilling anger in Caleb's eyes when he'd found Cooper pinning her to the cot.

Held in two men's arms in less than ten minutes time, yet each with such different intent. She shivered again at the taste of Cooper's brutality, fingering her swollen lower lip.

Sighing, she leaned into the evergreen branches, imagining they were Caleb's strong, protective arms. The thought fanned a fire in her belly as sure as the open flue pulled sparks from coal.

Thank You, Lord, for being my first protector. But thank You, too, for sending Caleb.

The back door shut, and her father stomped his feet before coming up front.

"It's snowing."

Annie turned toward the window. Penny-size flakes fell from the gray sky and settled on the boardwalk. Dry and crisp, they held their starry shapes instead of melting like the first snow back home in Omaha.

"Oh, Daddy, it's beautiful."

"It's also cold," he said, brushing the white dust from his shoulders. "Let's get this tree set and I'll stoke the fire. It's going to be a cold one tonight."

Grateful to be in the store and not the livery, Annie prayed that Caleb would be warm and dry in the box stall. Maybe she should take him another quilt. With the down from their Christmas goose, plus what she'd gathered at the river, she could start a feather cover for him. She would let Martha know, too, and maybe barter for enough down to finish one this winter.

Warmth flooded her neck. Such a thought for a single woman to have.

Her father laid the tree flat on the floor, held a squared wooden cross against the cut edge and positioned a large nail in the center.

With two swift hammer hits, he drove the nail head flush to the wood.

"Imagine," she said. "A cross and nails at Christmas holding everything together."

Caleb's confession came to mind and sadness engulfed her. A bittersweet recognition that he must follow God's leading—even if it took him away from Cañon City.

Away from her.

Her father raised the tree to stand straight and tall. Annie slipped an arm around his waist. "Thank you."

"We'd better get some corn popping so you can start on a garland for the tree. If you're feeling all right, Annie. Do you need to see the doctor?" he asked, his gaze falling to her bruised mouth.

"No, Daddy, I'm fine. I promise."

She wasn't as fine as she wanted to be and her lip stung where it had cut on her teeth. She still felt Cooper's weight pressing her down, and if she could, she'd strip off the dress she wore and burn it in the stove. Burn away the memory of his sour breath and rough hands.

But right now she had to put on a good face for her father.

Just then, the bell clanged as the Smiths poured through the door, bundled and stomping and laughing. The children's eyes glittered like Christmas candles when they saw the stately pine.

"Oh, Mama. It smells so pretty. Can we have a tree?" Emmy Smith tugged at her mother's skirt. "Can you buy one from Mr. Wicker for us?"

Louisa Smith laughed and knelt beside her daughter. "Where would we put a tree in our tiny cabin?"

Emmy's lower lip quivered, and her blue eyes pooled with enough tears to set Annie's father astir.

"I know just where you can get a tree for your home." He threw an exaggerated wink at Springer, who stood behind his mother and sister, failing to hide the yearning in his own eyes.

"Just this morning I saw one that could sit on a tabletop. Just right for a pint like you." He patted Emmy's head, and she tucked her chin.

"I ain't no pint."

"You *aren't* a pint," Louisa corrected.

Emmy stomped her little foot. "That's what I said."

Annie stifled a laugh and moved behind the counter. Did she look like that when she stomped her foot?

Annie's father drew something from his pocket and slipped it to Springer with a whisper and a nod. An over-size grin spread across the boy's face, and he tugged his hat and addressed his mother. "I'll be right back. Got an errand to run."

"Hurry," she said. "I want to be home in this storm, not out stuck somewhere in a snowdrift." Louisa pegged Annie's father with a merry frown that twitched her lips into a smile. "You're going to spoil us all, Daniel Whitaker."

Louisa shuttled Emmy to the table to look through a button box, then returned to the counter and lowered her voice. "I'd like to see your calico, please."

Annie laid a sky-blue cloth on the counter. A dress for Emmy, no doubt. Aunt Harriet wouldn't be fingering calico for a Christmas gift, nor would her sister, Edna. In fact, Edna was probably up to her ringlets in ruffles and lace planning the perfect dress for her spring wedding.

With no warning, Annie saw herself in a beautiful wedding dress with Caleb awaiting her in the church, but the startling image fled as suddenly as it had appeared.

"Annie?"

Roused from her daydream, she focused again on her customer. "I'm sorry. I was just thinking about...your cabin.

You said you had a cabin. So you are out of the tent in time for winter?"

"Yes." Louisa sighed with appreciation. "My William worked so hard to get it completed, and the Turk brothers helped, bless their souls. It's not big, but it's so much warmer with the fireplace and all."

It didn't take much for Annie to imagine herself at home in a small cabin with...

The bell over the door rang, and Emmy's two small hands clapped her cheeks, her mouth a rosebud O.

Springer held a perfect little sapling in his hands. "Just right, don't you think, Ma?"

Annie reached for a skein of red ribbon, snipped off a generous length and rolled and tucked it inside the Smiths' package.

"For hanging the stars and gingerbread men," she whispered to Louisa.

Annie watched the family hurry through the falling snow, wondering what it would be like to hurry home with Caleb.

Chapter 13

Caleb encouraged Cooper through the magistrate's door and waited for Frank Warren to draw his long, lean body out of the chair by the woodstove. More cabin than jail, the room housed a cage in the back for holding offenders until the people's court met to decide what to do with them.

A frown creased the magistrate's brow as he gave the saloon owner a quick once-over, pausing on the man's blood-stained brocade vest.

"I found him taking liberties at Whitaker's Mercantile that were completely unacceptable." Caleb tugged his hat down and stepped back, distancing himself from the scoundrel before giving into the urge for further action.

"And what were you doing at the mercantile, Cooper?" Warren folded his arms and sat on the edge of his desk.

"Can't a man make a friendly call on the local shopkeeper?"

Caleb took a step forward and Warren stopped him with a glare.

"And that shopkeeper would be Daniel Whitaker?"

Cooper fussed and flustered and mumbled something about the Whitaker woman being excessively unfriendly.

Caleb didn't know if he could control himself.

Warren ambled across the open space and escorted the bloodied saloon owner to the back corner. Cooper twisted in the magistrate's grip. "I'll see you pay for this," he shouted at Caleb.

"Keep your threats to yourself, Cooper." Warren locked the door and pocketed the key. Three long strides returned him to the stove's warmth, where he lowered his voice. "Those liberties happen to involve a Miss Annie Whitaker?"

Caleb's blood heated. "I figured murder was a hanging offense even this far west, so I brought him to you instead."

Warren's sweeping mustache quirked with apparent appreciation of Caleb's self-restraint. "Court meets day after tomorrow. We'll hold the old cuss here until then."

Warren crossed the room, took a seat behind a broad oak desk and opened a ledger. "This isn't the first report we've had of him taking a shine to the single womenfolk, but you're the first witness we've had to the offense, other than the women themselves."

"Will there be a trial?"

"More likely an informal hearing." Warren's gaze shifted from the ledger to Caleb's reddened knuckles. "I take it you're the one responsible for the bloodletting?"

"Yes, sir." Caleb flexed his fingers, swollen now from the force of his fist coming to blows with Cooper's nose.

"Any other witnesses?"

"Just myself and Ann—Miss Whitaker, but I saw to it that Cooper apologized to her father, who returned to the store not long after the incident."

Warren grunted his approval. "Good. A confession. That

will speed things right along. I'd just as soon get Cooper out of these parts, and this might do it. Time he sold to somebody respectable and moved on."

He laid his pen down and leaned back in the squeaky chair. "In fact, I think I know someone who might be interested in buying the hotel and saloon. Give Cooper a stake to leave and clean up the town all at the same time."

Caleb reset his hat. "I work at the livery. I'd appreciate a word about the hearing before it takes place."

"Oh, you'll hear," Warren said. "Court meets in Cooper's building, upstairs above the saloon. You might even be called on to testify."

Caleb nodded his thanks and opened the door.

"Good timing," Warren said.

Pausing, Caleb looked over his shoulder into the magistrate's coal-chip eyes.

"Good thing you happened by the mercantile when you did."

A tight throat and tighter chest prevented Caleb from speaking before he stepped onto the boardwalk and closed the door.

In spite of the drop in temperature, Caleb smoldered with the closest he'd ever come to righteous anger. *Lord, vengeance is Yours, You say...*

A sudden wind whipped down the street, swirling giant snowflakes into his face. He screwed his hat down, turned up his collar and shoved his hands into his pockets. He had to go check on Annie, to make sure she was all right and to let her know she need not worry about Jedediah Cooper, seeing as how he was now locked up.

After scouting both ways along Main Street, he bent his head against the wind and crossed the frozen roadway. A large evergreen filled the mercantile's front window, and a dozen such trees from his childhood paraded across his memory. As he reached for the knob, the door flew open and his young friend Springer darted out with a miniature tree, his sister chasing close behind. Caleb stepped back and tugged his hat brim to Springer's mother, who quickly followed, arms heaped high with wrapped bundles.

"Can I help you, Mrs. Smith?"

Tired but smiling blue eyes met his for a moment before latching on to running children. "Thank you, but I've got help aplenty—if I can just catch it."

The woman dashed down the boardwalk as if a child herself. Springer had already tossed the tree into a nearby buckboard and was lifting his giggling sister in. He relieved his mother of her armload, then helped her to the seat before climbing in and gathering the reins.

The family scene clutched at Caleb's heart. Would he ever know such blessings?

"Well, are you coming in or are you going to stand there until you look like a snowman?" Annie stood in the doorway with her hands on her hips.

He stomped his boots on the walk and stepped inside, wondering which he was more grateful for—the inviting warmth of the mercantile or the beautiful woman who worked there.

He slapped the snow from his hat and smiled into gold-flecked eyes. "Don't mind if I do."

She laid a hand on his sleeve when she caught sight of his knuckles. "Is your hand all right?"

The heat from her touch shot through him, and he struggled to speak for a moment. "No need to worry about me, Annie. It's you I'm concerned about."

Daniel tossed two coal chunks in the stove, shut the belly's door and clapped black dust off his hands. "Looks like we're about to have the first good storm of the season."

Responsibility pulled Caleb's attention to the windows.

Snowfall had thickened in a matter of moments, and it covered the boardwalk with a downy blanket. From what he'd heard of Rocky Mountain blizzards, he should leave now for the livery and check the stock before the storm worsened.

"Surely you'll stay and have a bite with us. Won't you, Caleb? I'm sure my father is as eager as I am to hear what happened with the magistrate."

A slight flush replaced Annie's pallor, and he ached to pull her into his arms again. Torn between duty and desire, he chose the latter, convincing himself that a quick meal, hot cup and good company would give him the sustenance he'd need to weather the storm in a stable.

"Let me take your hat while you warm yourself at the stove. And I'll have the stew heated in no time."

He followed her with his eyes and watched her assign his worn felt to a peg on the back wall. Daniel filled a tin mug and raised it in Caleb's direction.

"Coffee's hot, son. Come have a cup."

Caleb took the mug and a chair and felt as naked as a jay under Daniel's sober scrutiny.

Caleb glanced at the tree. "That's quite a spruce you've got there, Mr. Whitaker."

"That it is," Whitaker said, lifting his gaze to the tall evergreen at the window. Sorrow slipped across his features, landing briefly in his eyes.

"That tree nearly cost me the most precious thing in my world." He blinked a time or two and rubbed the back of his hand beneath his nose.

"Now, Daddy." Annie tightened her apron sash and gathered tin plates from the sideboard. "We've the good Lord to thank and Caleb here." She shot a bright look his way.

Caleb smiled at her, unaware that he was fingering the hole worn in the elbow of his shirt. When her eyes landed there, he pulled his hand away, but Annie was already talking to her father.

"Daddy, I believe Caleb could use some help with a new shirt." A look passed between them that Caleb didn't quite understand.

Daniel's watery eyes took in Caleb's cotton shirt, and he pushed out of the chair with a grunt. "I've got a wool shirt that might fit you. And good cloth that Martha could sew up in no time."

Caleb set his cup beneath his chair and followed Daniel to the front. The storekeeper reached under the counter and pulled out two waistcoats, heavy socks and a deep blue wool shirt that probably cost half the wages Caleb had managed to save.

He fingered the dark wool, felt the promise of warmth and knew he'd be a fool not to buy it. He set it aside and pulled the notepaper and *Cañon City Times* from his waistcoat and laid them on top. Then he unbuttoned a heavier tweed waistcoat that looked like it fit and exchanged it for the lighter one he wore. Already he felt better knowing he'd sleep warmer tonight beneath the quilt and canvas.

"I'll take this waistcoat and the shirt," he said, digging his money from the old waistcoat pocket. "And a soap bar, if you've got it."

Daniel reached into a box shelved halfway up the wall. "If you need it, we've got it." Then he tore a large square of brown paper from a roll on the counter, laid the shirt and Caleb's old waistcoat in the center and topped it with the soap and two pairs of heavy socks before wrapping it all together with twine.

"That'll be two dollars." A cocked brow dared an argument.

Caleb laid his money on the counter, fully aware that Daniel Whitaker was giving him five dollars' worth of merchandise, at least by Saint Joseph standards. It was all probably worth a lot more out here, but he'd not assault the man's dignity by arguing.

"Thank you."

Daniel's mustache twitched on his kindly face, and Caleb thought of Saint Nicholas, but a sadder saint this time.

"I'll leave this here until I go."

"Go? We've got a tree to decorate and I can use all the help I can get stringing chokecherries and popcorn."

Annie stood before the stove, a plate in each hand, loose hair curling against her neck—the most beautiful sight Caleb had set eyes on in his entire life.

"You hear that?" Daniel blew his nose and returned the handkerchief to his back pocket. "You'll not get away without poking a hole in every one of your fingers."

Caleb laughed but glanced out the window at the steadily falling snow. He'd stay just long enough to eat and then get back to the livery.

Returning to his chair, Caleb accepted the heaped plate Annie offered and waited until she had seated herself between her father and him.

Daniel bowed his head and began nearly before his daughter had settled.

"Thank You, Lord, for protecting my Annie." His voice cracked, and he paused to clear his throat. "And thank You for sending Caleb when You did and for this food and the strong roof over our heads. Amen."

The memory of Annie pinned beneath Cooper pushed itself unwelcomed into Caleb's mind. He forced his thoughts instead to the stately spruce in the store window and last year's tree in the parsonage decorated by the Women's Society. Glittering guilt tried to top the pine, but he doggedly knocked it away and replaced it with gratitude.

Cañon City might just be where he belonged. For what

reason he wasn't yet sure, but he hoped it had something to do with a certain storekeeper's auburn-haired daughter.

Annie pushed hard against the door after Caleb left. Thin powder drifted through a gap at the bottom and swirled against her shoes. She hugged her arms across her chest and watched until he disappeared into the blowing snow. Without his duster he'd be frozen solid by the time he made it to the livery. Thank goodness she'd given him another quilt before he left.

She began to shiver and retreated to the stove. Her father sat sipping his coffee and staring at the potbelly. She had to get his mind off the Cooper incident—for her sake as well as his.

Caleb had assured them that the people's court would meet soon to deal with Cooper. At least that was what the magistrate had promised.

Annie had made the acquaintance of several men who served on the court—upstanding citizens who often visited when they came for their mail or shared coffee round the stove. Edna had been right about one thing: there was no law in Cañon City. At least not like they had in Omaha. No sheriff or marshal yet, but these men didn't seem to brook much nonsense. She'd already seen a couple of scoundrels run out of town, and she prayed the same fate would befall Jedediah Cooper.

She filled the dishpan from a crock by the wall and set it on the stove. Gazing at the beautiful spruce in the window, she tried to shift her thoughts to Christmas, which was only two weeks away. Oh, for the delicate ornaments that adorned Aunt Harriet's tree, and the crèche that held the highest honor on the mantel. Mary, Joseph and baby Jesus tucked into the stable—

With a jolt Annie thought of the livery and Nell. She

hadn't checked on the mare in several days, and she'd forgotten to ask Caleb about her condition.

What if Nell foaled during the storm? And needed help?

Caleb was there.

Relief nestled in her thoughts. He knew what to do.

Warmth threaded through her arms, and she doubted it came from the water bubbling in the dishpan. She shaved in soap curls and from the corner of her eye noted her father's pensive mood.

"As soon as this weather lets up, we could invite Martha and Caleb and the Smiths over for a tree trimming. What do you think?"

Her father let out a deep sigh, then stood and added his cup to the dishpan. "I think that's a fine idea, Annie girl. A fine idea." He planted a kiss on her cheek and twisted the end of his mustache. Turning his back to the stove, he clasped both hands behind him and looked through the front windows.

"I doubt we'll have any more customers today," he said.

Annie scrubbed the plates. "I'm sure glad Nell's in a safe, warm place." Her heart fluttered like a sparrow at her throat, but she pressed on. "I've been meaning to tell you, but Nell's in a…"

Waiting for the right words to form on her lips, Annie gathered her skirt in her hands, lifted the dishpan from the stove and set it on the back counter.

"In a what? A stall? 'Course she is, and I still don't think it's worth what I'm paying to board her. Can't sell her now, but come spring, I'm sure the Turks or Deacons will offer a good price."

Annie's pulse quickened, but she straightened her back and lifted her chin. "She's in a family way, Daddy. She's carrying a foal."

His gasp sucked the air from the back of the store, and

Annie clamped her mouth tight to guard her own desperate breath.

"How long have you known?"

She glanced over her shoulder. Surprise, rather than anger, rimmed his eyes.

"Caleb told me. I'd thought she was just getting a hay belly, but he said he expects her to foal sometime around Christmas."

If she phrased it right, she might still turn things around. She shook her hands over the dishpan and rubbed them against her apron before joining her father at the stove.

"Isn't it wonderful, Daddy? A Christmas foal. A new little life in the stable, just like—"

He pulled her into a hug and kissed the top of her head. "I feel you twisting me around your finger, Annie Whitaker."

He chuckled, and the laughter shook her as he held her close.

"But I guess it's as Martha says—the more the merrier."

Gratitude filled Annie's heart, and she inched back from her father's embrace. "Speaking of Martha, is there anything you'd like to tell *me?*"

Her father harrumphed and sputtered and flushed from his collar to his snowy crown. But his eyes took on a mischievous gleam, and he pinched Annie's chin like he had when she was little.

"Don't avoid the subject, Daddy. Will there be a wedding this spring instead of a horse sale?"

His full-bellied laugh bounced Annie from his arm and she sent a silent thank-you heavenward.

"How did you know?"

"I'd have to be blind and deaf not to." Annie returned to the dishpan. She'd worry about details later—details like living alone in the back room once her father moved into

Martha's home. Right now she wanted to share his good news with a clear heart.

"I'm not blind, either, Annie girl."

She looked up from the water.

"What happened at the livery?"

She rested her hands on the edge of the dishpan, noting her father's calculating expression. He knew.

"How long have you known?"

He smoothed his mustache and sat down. "He told me a couple of weeks ago, but I suspected early on. Remember the morning I asked him to offer thanks? A prayer like that comes from a man who's on a first-name basis with the Lord."

She picked up a plate and absently rubbed a cloth against its clean surface. "I think he'll be returning to his calling." Sadness gripped her belly, followed by regret that she would react so. She should be happy for Caleb, that he'd found his way back to the Lord and his life's purpose.

But where did that leave her?

The front door rattled in a sudden forceful gust, and concern needled Annie. She looked to the half-empty coal bucket and back to the door, where a fine white powder swirled in eddies along the floor.

Her father shrugged into his coat and headed toward the back door with the coal bucket. "Find towels for the doors and I'll bring in more coal. We'll probably need a full fire going all day and night."

Annie knelt at the trunk and withdrew thick blankets and fine linens intended for the table, not the floor. But they had no table, and staying warm was a priority. Aunt Harriet would be appalled.

At the thought of her proud and proper relative, Annie's heart squeezed with longing for her sister. And though she missed her sibling desperately, for the first time in her life she was grateful for their satin and calico differences. Grateful that she didn't panic before a howling blizzard and the possibility of being snowbound for days. Grateful that God had brought her and her father safely to Cañon City, to people like the Smith family and Martha Bobbins and…

And Caleb Hutton.

With this wind, she easily imagined snow blowing through the slatted stable walls. Nell wasn't the only one she prayed would be safe and dry and warm during the storm.

She tossed extra blankets on the cots and took two finely hand-stitched dish towels to the front, where she weighted them against the door with flatirons. Not exactly the way she'd planned to use those embroidered dish towels from her hope chest, but at least she had them to use.

Be grateful for small blessings.

Indeed. Annie would not trade this narrow store and potbelly stove for all the finery and wealthy beaus Omaha could offer. Here she belonged.

And here she would stay.

Caleb dropped his bundle by the stable doors and ran to bring Rooster and Sally inside. Shouldering all his weight against the broad panels, he managed to close them against the wind before too much snow blew into the alleyway.

He led his horses to the last two empty stalls and tossed them each an armful of hay. Unsettled by the creaking rafters and whistling walls, a few of his charges blew and stamped nervously. Nell dozed in the ruckus, one back leg cocked at the knee and her eyes half-closed.

Caleb heaved a heavy sigh. At least there'd be no delivery tonight.

He pitched his bundle and the new quilt onto the bedroll, rousing the cat from her tight curl. She blinked once, stretched her toothy mouth in a wide yawn and recoiled herself against the quilt.

Annie's quilt.

He knew because he'd held it to his face all the way back from the mercantile, breathing in her lovely scent. Did she really care that much about his well-being, care that he was warm during the storm?

Henry had a fire in his forge, bless him, but he must have gone home to ride out the storm with his wife. The thought set a yearning inside Caleb stout enough to push him out into the wind and back to the mercantile. But what would he say? *Marry me, Annie. Come live in the livery and be my wife.*

The sheer audacity of such a proposal embarrassed him. It would be a long while before he shared anything more than a simple meal with Annie Whitaker.

He'd not ask her to share his life until he knew where and what that life would be.

He unwrapped his bundle, tucked the soap in his pocket and took his water bucket to Henry's furnace along with his new shirt. In the fire's radiant warmth, he washed, then exchanged his thin cotton shirt for the new dark wool, grateful for the comfort and the fit. Whitaker was right.

Back in his stall, Caleb lit the lamp and unfolded the *Times*. The main article was about the rise and progress of Cañon City. It mentioned all the buildings that were going up and how the city had weathered the "calamity that disheartened gold seekers had thrown upon it."

Caleb set the paper aside and lay back on his bedroll. Gold seekers weren't the only disheartened souls who had sought out this far Kansas Territory. He reached for his Bible and let it fall open. Jeremiah again, the weeping prophet, and Mollie Sullivan's picture. He studied the image of the woman smiling up from between the pages.

Pretty, yes. Beguiling, certainly. A woman after his heart? Not at all. Never had been, he realized now.

He took the Bible to Henry's forge, where the fire lay dying in a cooling bank. With no malice or ill thoughts, he laid Mollie's picture against a fading coal. "Bless her, Lord. And may she and her husband serve You."

The copper-edged image curled and shriveled to ash as he watched, and he sensed a small flame purging a place deep in his soul. He looked at the passage he had long ago marked in the nineteenth chapter of Jeremiah. The fire's dim glow hardly illuminated the page, but the words had taken up residence in his memory.

"For I know the thoughts that I think toward you, saith the Lord, thoughts of peace and not of evil, to give you an expected end."

The promised peace settled like a cloak around him. Outside the wind beat against the livery, and the building groaned in the onslaught. He wrapped his arms around his chest and held the book within them. Finally, after months of running, here in a barn, he could rest in God's expected end. Not what he, Caleb, had expected, but what the Lord knew He had planned.

With a deep sense of surrender, Caleb returned to the box stall, snuffed out the lamp and crawled beneath his canvas tarp, Annie's quilts and the enduring grace of a loving God.

Chapter 14

A blue china sky greeted Annie Sunday morning, the air as crisp and cold as deep well water. White drifts leaned against the Main Street buildings, and the roadway was a frozen, mudless track. In Omaha a storm like yesterday's would have her sister and their aunt soaking dirty skirt hems after church for sure. Not to mention their fine cloth shoes.

She snugged her scarf closer and waited on the boardwalk for her father.

Only the Lord's Day could still the perpetual hammering of the city's rising. Though the community stretched and fussed with growing pains, life was simpler in this bare-bones mountain supply town. Her heart felt lighter knowing she didn't have to compete with Edna's fashionable clothing or cringe beneath Aunt Harriet's glaring judgment of unruly hair.

Annie knew she fell short of her aunt's expectations,

particularly where men were concerned. Not that Cañon City was teeming with eligible bachelors worth even a second glance. Most were lonely miners who drank too much, dusty cowboys in need of a good bath or entrepreneurs who knew a good investment when they saw one.

Or a gentle horse handler who continued to occupy her thoughts and warm her heart. She took a forceful breath of sharp air to clear her mind.

"Ready, Annie girl?"

Her father shut the mercantile door and offered his arm. Grateful for the short walk to the church house, she curved her fingers inside his elbow. Buggies and buckboards lined the street beyond the church, and a few horses stood loosely tied to the livery's hitching rail across the way, a location upon which her eyes so easily settled.

The big front doors parted just enough for a peek into the shadowy stable. Heat wrapped around her neck at the thought of Caleb beneath her quilts, and she banished the vision with a quick prayer that he'd been warm and safe through the storm.

Annie hiked her skirt to mount the church steps. Hannah Baker was not at her usual post at the door with her soon-to-be husband, Pastor Hartman. Surely a brisk winter storm had not been too much for the rancher's daughter, always cheerful as a meadowlark, greeting everyone with her melodic voice and bright smile.

Annie hurried inside. Hannah sat slump-shouldered halfway to the front, wilting beneath a woolen scarf and dabbing at her cheeks, cloistered by her family. Annie and her father found a bench a few rows back and soon learned the sad truth. Pastor Hartman took to the pulpit, announcing that the couple's pending marriage the week after Christmas had been postponed indefinitely. His brother, Reverend Justice Hartman of Denver, had broken his leg in a buggy accident earlier in the month and word had just arrived that he dare not make the trip south to perform the ceremony.

In fact, he'd sent for Robert to officiate over Christmas festivities in Denver.

What arrogance. How dare the elder reverend presume upon his sibling and this fledgling community. Just because Justice Hartman's congregation had a fine brick building with a bell tower didn't mean he could drag Cañon City's beloved pastor from his flock.

But apparently blood was thicker than water—especially at Christmas. No wedding before the New Year. And unless someone stepped forward, no Christmas Eve services for the town's small congregation of merchants and miners and ranchers. The pastor's tone made it clear that he had bowed to his brother's wishes and would be leaving that very afternoon.

Annie nearly cried herself as she filed out with others after the service. This was not the Christmas she'd hoped for. Truth be told, she wasn't sure what she had hoped for in the first place. There would be no traditional trimmings she'd grown up with, no Edna or Harriet, no festivities at all—other than what she cobbled together at the mercantile. And now, no Christmas Eve service with carol singing and warm wishes from friends and— Oh—it just wasn't fair.

Her foot ached to stomp, and she held it to the wooden step and leaned her weight into it. She hadn't even had the small pleasure of speaking with Caleb.

Was he worried over Nell?

Annie's father spoke quietly in Pastor Hartman's ear, and both men looked out toward the livery.

Of course.

She snugged her cloak tighter and looked around for Martha. The seamstress stood commiserating with Hannah, and guilt's cold fingers clutched Annie's conscience for thinking only of herself and her own disappointment.

She approached with an outstretched hand. "I'm so sorry, Hannah." She squeezed the young woman's arm, which brought fresh tears. "I'm sure things will work out. He'll be back as soon as he can—you know he will."

If it didn't snow three feet between Christmas and January, like every freighter said it always did.

Turning to Martha, Annie lowered her voice. "Please tell Daddy I'll be along directly. I'm going to stop at the livery and check on Nell."

Martha's sorrowful eyes transformed. "You tell that young Caleb that we expect him for Sunday dinner. I've already set a place for him at the table."

Annie planted a kiss on Martha's cheek, squeezed Hannah's soggy handkerchief-wrapped fingers one more time and hurried across the road.

The perfume of sweet hay and horseflesh wafted from the stable as Annie squeezed between the doors. Had Christ's birthplace smelled like this? She'd never considered the possibility since every holiday season in her aunt's home smelled of baking and spices and candles and greenery. But here, in the shadowy stalls and open livery rafters, she felt somehow closer to the essence of the first Christmas.

Caleb's low voice sounded from Nell's stall and sent shivers up Annie's arms. She moved closer, watching him work his way behind the mare, his deep tones as comforting as a mother's lullaby. Annie held a hand to her mouth, afraid for even the quietest word to disturb the moment.

Caleb had rolled up his shirtsleeves, and his muscled forearms bore evidence of hard work. Annie knew the strength in those hands, but they smoothed along Nell's swelling body as gently as a flannel blanket. She knew that touch, as well, and it wakened something lying deep within her.

The memory of Caleb's rescue flooded her with warmth, and she shifted, drawing his attention outside the stall.

"It won't be long," he said softly.

Apparently satisfied with his charge's condition, he ducked beneath Nell's neck and gently opened the stall door. Standing close in the alleyway, he rolled down his sleeves and searched Annie's face in the most disarming way.

Grateful to be in shadow, she loosened her scarf. "You might want to pray that she foals soon, because I think you're about to be asked to fill in for Pastor Hartman for a while."

Caleb's expression sobered. "What makes you say that?"

"The pastor's brother in Denver was injured and won't be coming down to perform the wedding. Instead, he's asked Pastor Hartman to come to Denver and take over duties there for Christmas. Not only will there not be a wedding here, there won't be a Christmas Eve service, either."

Annie's sense of injustice had twisted the scarf she fingered into a knot. Caleb stared at her.

He hadn't made the connection. "I believe Daddy told the pastor of your previous calling."

Caleb finished rolling his sleeves down, buttoned his cuffs and reached for his hat. A sharp downward pull hid his eyes, and Annie took a step closer, seeking their depths. "You'll do it if they ask you, won't you?"

His embattled expression gave her pause, and she drew back. He stopped her with a hand at her waist and closed the distance between them.

Annie's heartbeat danced at her temple and in her throat. How dark his eyes were, as if he warred against some inner torment. She clutched the ends of her scarf in one hand and laid the other against his chest. His heart ran as hard as her own. "Do you doubt that you can do it?"

With his free hand, he touched her hair, then smoothed the back of his fingers against her cheek.

"You are beautiful, Annie Whitaker. Beautiful in spirit and in form."

She breathed in, commanding her breath to come evenly, steadily. It wouldn't do to swoon in his arms right there in the livery. Lowering her gaze, she studied the texture of his new waistcoat, at a loss for words for the first time in her life.

Caleb lifted her hand from his chest and pressed her fingers against his lips before putting a safer distance between them. "I can do it if He calls me."

Annie's heart hitched. "Pastor Hartman?"

He smiled at her confusion. "If God calls me. He'll enable me."

"But didn't He already call you?" She regretted her remark even as it slid from her lips, for sadness washed over his face. Without thinking, she reached to smooth it away.

He caught her hand. "Will you be there?"

"Yes." Would she ever breathe again without her heart racing like a runaway horse?

His smile returned, and he squeezed her hand and released it. "If God wants me to stand in His pulpit again, He'll make it clear to me and present the opportunity Himself."

Stunned by his humility and flushed with emotion, Annie moved toward the door, seeking the clarity of the cold air. "Martha is expecting you for dinner. She's already set a plate for you at the table."

His features softened, and he pulled his duster from a nail on the wall. "Then we'd best be going, hadn't we?"

He offered her his arm, and she couldn't help the smile that came to her face.

She took it without hesitation.

With Annie's hand tucked beneath his, Caleb counted calendar days in his head. A week and a half until Christmas Eve, with a Sunday service before that. Annie's news had simply confirmed his recent commitment. He'd already told the Lord he'd go where he was called.

Clattering hooves drew his attention to a cloaked rider approaching with his hat pulled low. Annie's fingers tightened on his arm.

"Caleb." Robert Hartman reined up beside them. "Annie." He touched his hat and his gray mount blew its smoky breath and stomped impatiently, invigorated by the cold and a promised run.

"Pastor Hartman," Caleb said. "We'll miss you at Christmas, but our prayers go with you for a safe trip to Denver."

"Thank you." Hartman yanked unnecessarily on the reins, sending the horse dancing backward. Caleb stepped forward and took the headstall, mumbling low.

"Annie's father tells me you're a preacher," the pastor said.

"Yes, sir. Spent a year or so at a small church in Missouri, then came west." With the flat of his hand he rubbed the horse's face while reading Hartman's expression. No need to go into reasons and regrets.

"Wish I'd known sooner. We could have visited, compared notes. But as you know, I'm on my way to my brother's and need someone to hold the Christmas Eve service that people are counting on. Not to mention next Sunday, and maybe more than that, depending. Are you willing?"

The gray startled forward at Hartman's clumsy kick, and the man jerked back on the reins again.

"Easy," Caleb murmured. Hartman's eagerness to leave transmitted to the horse. Caleb stepped aside. "I'd be happy to. Thank you for your trust."

The gray reared slightly and tossed its head. "I'll be back as soon as I can, and will send a letter to Hannah telling her when to expect my return."

Hartman looked at Annie. "Thank your father for me. I feel better knowing someone will be here in my absence." He nodded to Caleb. "I'll be praying for you."

"And I for you," Caleb said as the gray seemed to tiptoe on the frozen street. "Let up on the reins and watch your heels, and he'll be easier to handle."

Hartman grinned. "Thanks. I might say the same about our unique congregants. Merry Christmas."

Winning the struggle, the gray wheeled and charged east out of town. Caleb snugged Annie's arm close against him. He already knew the text for his message.

Two blocks west and they stepped off the boardwalk and turned north toward Martha's home. The dry snow squeaked beneath Caleb's boots and powdery crystals swirled in a light crosswind. Annie tucked her scarf against her chin.

Martha's walkway had been swept clear, and smoke curled from the chimney. Caleb opened the door for Annie, and his mouth watered at the aroma that welcomed them. After stomping his feet, he stepped in and closed the door. The small cabin swelled with goodwill and good food.

He'd gladly live in a cabin like this if Annie shared it with him.

He took Annie's cloak from her tense shoulders, wishing he could wrap her in his arms until she relaxed against him. Suspecting he knew the cause of her tension, he leaned close to her ear. "It's all right," he said. "Cooper won't hurt you again."

The look she gave him drew every ounce of protectiveness up through his veins. He wanted to keep her safe, warm, close.

God help him.

On Monday morning the hall above the Fremont Saloon overflowed with people for Cooper's hearing. Word got around fast.

Caleb stood against the back wall, a position that gave him a clear view of Cooper, Magistrate Warren and Annie seated with her father toward the front.

The saloon owner wasn't as cocky as he'd been the day Caleb dragged him to the jail. He was probably sober—a frightening condition for a man given to liquor and license.

Caleb wished there was some other way to go about justice that didn't require Annie's public testimony, but she held her head high and spoke clearly and unemotionally.

Cooper squirmed in his seat and the truth was apparent, if the murmurs and nods rippling through the crowd were any indication. Warren must have been right. It seemed that Cooper was overdue for his comeuppance.

After a brief discussion, the court members told Cooper that if he sold his property and left town immediately, they'd let him go. Otherwise, he'd serve time in jail and be required to pay a heavy fine. Caleb felt they were letting the man off too easy, but one look at Annie reminded him that Cooper's absence was what she really wanted.

The need to protect her surged through his blood again. Whatever it took.

The gavel sounded and Cooper was led away to turn over the deed to his hotel and saloon and ride out of town.

It was done. Now Caleb could spend the next few days preparing for his return to the pulpit.

Chapter 15

Caleb started a fire in the woodstove, lit the lamps and set out extra tapers for the Christmas Eve service. Then he swept the front steps and carried in the heap of pine boughs Karl Turk had earlier dropped by from his cuttings. Several branches still bore cones, and their sweet pitch filled the clapboard building with a familiar Christmas promise.

Fresh hope. A future. God's expected end.

Caleb longed for all three.

His first Sunday had gone well. People had not stayed away simply because their pastor was gone.

Humbled by Hartman's willingness to leave his flock in Caleb's care, and the congregation's willingness to give Caleb a chance, he checked the fire again and adjusted the damper. The small building should be warm by the time people arrived for the evening's service.

But rather than stay and go over his brief sermon, Caleb answered the tug on his heart that called him back to the livery. He'd learned a long time ago to follow that call where animals were concerned. He just hadn't paid it as much heed with people.

Scanning the room and pleased with his preparations, he softly closed the door and hurried to the livery.

Thank God he'd listened.

Nell flattened her ears as Caleb entered the stall—not her usual easygoing welcome. Her rounded belly had a more angular look, and she swished her tail and stomped a back foot. Caleb's gut twisted at the signs. Not *now*.

Agitated, Nell's discomfort sent her head reaching back toward her sides, blowing and whiffling. Caleb had no way to predict how soon or how quickly she would foal, and he couldn't be two places at once—in the livery with Nell and across the street at the Christmas Eve service.

He'd promised Hartman he'd care for the congregation— the brave souls who'd left the comforts and customs of home to start a new life in the Rockies. Maybe he could leave Nell to her own devices. How many times as a boy had he been surprised to walk in on a spindly legged foal nuzzling a carefree mama who had delivered without anyone's help?

But one never knew for sure. And Nell was Annie's joy. There was more to this delivery than simply another foal.

With divided loyalty tearing at his gut, he grabbed his duster and set out for the mercantile. The sliver of daylight above Fremont Peak told him folks would soon be arriving. He'd ask Annie and her father to watch Nell while he greeted people at the church and let him know if she was in distress. Annie stood bundled at the stove, ready to leave, while her father banked the fire and set the lid. The bell pulled her toward the door, and her eyes warmed with welcome until she saw what lay behind Caleb's own.

Hurrying to him, her voice was tight and worried. "What is it? Is something wrong at the church house?"

He clasped both her hands in his, regretting the tension he'd set in her brow. "It's Nell. She's close to her time."

He looked over Annie's head to her father tugging on his overcoat and scarf.

"I'm here to ask if you'll stay with her while I start the service and let the people know what's happening."

"Of course we will," Daniel said. "Let's go." He stormed out the door as if he'd put all his life and soul into that mare rather than bemoan her appetite.

The lantern Caleb had hung outside Nell's stall pooled a yellow light in the alleyway and deepened the shadows beyond. Nell whinnied at the intrusion and flattened her ears in warning.

"Don't go in," Caleb said. "No matter what happens, do not go in the stall."

Annie and Daniel leaned against the railing, looking as if they'd never seen a horse in all their lives. Maybe this wasn't such a good idea.

"Promise me." Caleb laid his hand on Annie's shoulder, pressing until she looked at him.

"I promise," she said.

Nell paced as much as the cramped box allowed, and Caleb wished he had a larger space for her. In her irritable condition, any unwelcome intruder could be hurt. Or killed.

"It's very likely she'll deliver without any problem. She may lie down and get up again. She may kick or moan. Whatever she does, do not go in there."

"What should we look for?" Daniel's steady voice and calm expression restored Caleb's confidence in his choice of guardian.

"Two hooves and a nose is what we want to come first." His discomfort at mentioning such intimate details in Annie's presence subsided as he studied her unflustered profile. "If anything else presents instead, come and get me."

She touched his arm. "Daddy will come and get us. I am going with you." Her fingers pressed into his sleeve, and she lowered her voice. "I will be praying for you as well as for Nell."

Caleb's heart hammered into his throat. With a final glance at the mare, and then at the lovely woman who believed in him more than he felt he deserved, he took her hand and they strode out the livery doors and across the street.

Hannah and her parents had driven in from their ranch, and Caleb gratefully acknowledged the young woman's tending of the lanterns and candles. The little church glowed with goodwill, and people chose benches closer to the front this evening, either to join in the festive Christmas spirit or to avoid the dropping temperature that lurked beyond the back door.

Caleb stepped up on the rough-hewn platform to lead the first carol.

No organ or piano accompanied the rich vocal mix of miner and merchant. But all knew the tune and those who were brave broke into harmony. The few children's angelic voices joined the chorus, and Caleb's spirit rose on the sound. The very angels who declared the Lord's birth could not have announced it more majestically than the simple folk of this little mountain town.

His eyes settled on Annie, seated with the Smith family. She caught his look and held it with what appeared to be a promise. Could she someday be his?

Warmed by the fire and the bodies crowded into the tiny church, the air simmered with paraffin, kerosene and fresh pine. Bible in hand, Caleb stood next to the simple pulpit, wanting nothing between him and the people this night.

"As you all know, I care for the stock at the livery—a skill I learned many years before my seminary training. I stand here this evening to extend to you your pastor's heartfelt Christmas blessings, to rejoice with you in our Lord's priceless gift and also to explain the situation at hand."

People settled in their places. Women removed their gloves, and men balanced hats on their laps.

Caleb cleared his throat and took a small step forward. "The Whitakers' mare has chosen this night to birth her foal, and if I'm needed—I apologize—but I'll be stepping out."

A few murmurs hummed across the room, but no one left. A good sign.

A deep breath loosened his chest, and the familiarity of God's word strengthened his stance. "The Scriptures tell us that our faith is more valuable than gold. We know something about that around here, don't we? *Gold.*"

His emphasis of the word set heads to wagging and eyes to glittering.

"Consider the gifts the Christ child received from the Eastern kings. Frankincense, myrrh, gold. A king's gold, pure and refined and weighty, nothing like what men scrabble for in the creek beds and canyons of these Rocky Mountains."

A few chuckles rippled across the room as men cast knowing glances among themselves and women *tsked.*

"So what kind of treasure do we bring to the babe this Christmas? Refined, pure gold or crusty ore mixed with pebbles and dirt?"

The question sobered his listeners, and he lifted his

Bible to read from First Peter. "'Wherein ye greatly rejoice, though now for a season, if need be, ye are in heaviness through manifold temptations.'"

He looked up from the page and into the eyes of those seated on the benches and standing against the walls. "We have manifold temptations represented here this evening. I personally have enough to pass among you with plenty left over. But I confess that I have not greatly rejoiced in them."

Again he lifted the book and read from it. "'That the trial of your faith, being much more precious than of gold that perisheth, though it be tried with fire, might be found unto praise and honor and glory at the appearing of Jesus Christ.'"

A chilly gust swept in and stilled Caleb's heart as he looked up to see Daniel at the door, worry tightening his brow. Annie looked toward the back, and sat straighter, as if ready to stand. "Prospectors and speculators will tell you there is no gold in Cañon City. Show them otherwise. Let the trial in your life—whatever that trial may be—purify your faith to a burning, burnished gold, worthy of the King who was the Child, so that something more valuable than mined mountain ore will shine for Him here."

He closed his Bible and looked over the celebrants. "With Mr. Whitaker's sudden arrival, it appears that I am needed at the stable."

Low voices buzzed, and most turned to look toward the entrance.

"I apologize for cutting this celebration short, but I wish you all a blessed Christmas and pray for your safe journey home and warm memories of your first such event in the great canyon's guardian city."

Hannah rose to attend to the candles and lanterns, and

Caleb thanked her as he grabbed his hat and duster and hurried out, Annie at his side.

The few lines that Annie heard Caleb speak revealed a side of him she longed to know more of. But right now, she needed the horseman, because Nell must be having a tough go of it.

Caleb stripped off his hat and coat as they entered the barn, gave them to Annie and rolled up his sleeves. Nell lay on her side and great rolling contractions rippled across her belly. Caleb eased into the stall, sending his rich, warm voice ahead. Nell's ears flicked his way and back again.

His gentle confidence stilled Annie's pounding heart, and she linked her arm through her father's. Within moments Caleb caught two tiny hooves with one hand and a white nose in the other. With one final heave, Nell pushed a new life into his arms.

The mare lay still, exhausted and breathing hard. Annie feared she had no strength left at all when the horse raised her head and curled back around to sniff and nicker a motherly welcome. Finally, she pulled herself up and turned to stand over the leggy infant, licking and rumbling deep in her chest.

Annie stood enthralled by what she saw, so much so that she didn't hear the great livery doors open and a small crowd approach. When a child's voice broke the stillness, she looked around to see a dozen people pressing into the alleyway, craning their necks for a look at the newborn.

"Welcome to Cañon City, little fella." Emmy Smith peeked through the stall slats at the wobbly foal, at its spindly legs fighting for purchase.

"I think you mean little *filly*," Caleb said with a smile in his voice.

Laughter rippled through the onlookers, and Emmy tucked her chin and poked out her lip.

"They're not laughing at you—they're laughing with you," Springer said, kneeling beside his sister. "It's a little girl. *Filly* means girl."

"Like me?" Emmy's bright eyes searched her papa's face, where he stood with an arm tightly about her mama's shoulders.

"That's right, darlin'. Just like you."

"Guess you knew what you were talkin' about, Hutton." The crusty voice rose from behind the crowd, and heads turned to identify the speaker.

Magistrate Warren cleared his throat and tugged at his hat. "There's more gold here in these hills than the kind that glitters."

The yellow filly hobbled forward and nuzzled her mother, and people jostled and bid each other "Merry Christmas" on their way out of the stable.

At last, only Annie, her father and Caleb stood at the gate watching Nell and her foal. Annie slipped an arm through that of each man standing beside her and pulled them closer.

"Imagine, spending Christmas Eve in a barn. What would Aunt Harriet say?"

Her father coughed out a laugh that startled the filly, and he clamped a hand over his mouth and stepped back.

Annie giggled and looked to Caleb, whose eyes held so much warmth and love that she wanted to melt into his arms right then and there.

"I'd best be getting to the mercantile," her father said. "Martha's there with a Christmas pudding waiting on us all to string popcorn for the tree."

Annie hugged his girth and planted a kiss on his cheek.

"You did a fine job tonight, son. A fine job." He slapped Caleb on the shoulder and headed for the door. "I'm going on. You both come along when you're finished here." He paused at the door. "You know you're invited, Caleb. We wouldn't have it any other way. The more the merrier."

Annie caught the twinkle in her father's eyes and swore she saw his mustache twitch.

Caleb retrieved a water bucket and towel from his living quarters and washed his arms and hands in the lantern's light. Annie looked away, warmth flooding her neck and cheeks. Such intimate moments they'd shared this day. What would Edna say?

She didn't care what Edna would say. Annie had found more in Cañon City than she'd ever dreamed. And she wasn't about to let proprieties take that from her.

With new resolve, she turned to see Caleb watching her, pulling on his duster and settling his hat on his head. An odd smirk played on his lips.

"What?" Suddenly fidgety, she swirled her scarf around her neck and dug in her cloak pocket for her mittens.

He moved toward her, and her feet grew roots. She couldn't have fled if she wanted to. But she *didn't* want to. His dark eyes drank her in in that disarming way, and she felt her insides go limp.

He stopped just beyond her tightly clutched hands, so close she felt his breath on her face, smelled the scent of him—the wool and leather, his canvas duster. He slipped one hand around her waist and pulled her into him, brushing her mouth with his eyes and then his lips.

She flattened both hands against his chest and again felt his heart beating a rhythm in time with her own.

"I love you, Annie Whitaker. Will you wait for me?"

Wait? What's to wait for?

She searched for her voice and found it snagged on her heart.

"Wait?" she whispered.

"Until I have something to offer you. A home. A liveli-hood. Something besides a stable boy's pay and a box stall."

Her voice fled again and tears pushed behind her eyes. She swiped at them, determined not to be a silly twit like her sister. With a shaky breath, she yanked her voice back from its hiding place.

"On one condition."

His eyes sparkled at her counter, and he pressed her closer. "And what might that be?"

"That you kiss me again right now before Daddy and Martha come looking for us."

He gave her a smile that nearly stopped her heart, and she melted into his embrace.

Epilogue

Annie fussed with her long buttoned sleeves and reset her hair combs for the hundredth time.

"Let me," Martha said, shooing Annie's hands away from her head. "Be still now. You look absolutely divine. I tell you, that young man of yours won't know his head from his hat when he sees you in this blue taffeta. I knew I'd have a need for it someday, and with your hair shining like a kiln fire, how will he ever concentrate enough to marry Hannah and Robert?"

Annie wrapped the seamstress in a quick hug, then allowed her to fuss over the folds of her skirt. Hannah watched them both with a nervous twitch that set her bouquet to quivering against her cream-colored gown.

"Oh, Hannah, you're not frightened, are you?" Annie held a hand out to the girl, who looked as if she might faint any moment.

"I'm just so nervous," Hannah whispered as if sharing

a secret. "I want everything to go right and be done with. Tell me again how this is all going to work."

"We're all going to be *Mrs.* to our dear husbands, child." Martha bloomed like a rose in her garden as she gave Annie's hair a final pat and turned to the youngest of the three brides. "You will lead us between the bench rows at the church house, followed by Annie and then myself. Your Robert, Annie's Caleb and my Daniel will be waiting for us at the front."

"Then Caleb will take you and Robert through your vows," Annie said, fluffing Hannah's full sleeves. "He's going to kiss you in front of everyone." She couldn't resist teasing.

Hannah went white. "Caleb's going to kiss me?"

Martha burst into laughter, and Annie colored with guilty regret. "No, silly. *Robert* is going to kiss you. After Caleb marries you both."

"Then you will step back, Robert will step forward and Caleb will take his place beside Annie for their vows," Martha explained.

Heat pulsed at Annie's throat, and she almost regretted her gown's low neckline.

"Who will marry you and Daniel?" Hannah asked Martha, the homemade flowers steadier in her hand with so many questions on her mind.

"Robert," Annie said. "He is the original pastor, and as his last duty here, he will have the honor of joining my father and Martha." She slipped her arm around the seamstress's waist and gave her a quick hug. "Thanks to you and your talents, we make three lovely brides. Who would have thought you could fashion flowers from ribbon and lace and fabric scraps?"

Martha blushed and waved away the remark, her cheeks

nearly matching the deep burgundy of her simple but finely pleated dress.

Annie walked to the mercantile door. It looked like the entire town was trying to squeeze into the clapboard church house. Three brides and their grooms would not be the only people standing for the ceremony.

Winter had calmed its blustery self just long enough for Pastor Hartman to return for his bride. Annie prayed for it to hold until their safe return to Denver, where Hartman would take over for his still-recovering brother.

How suddenly circumstances had changed. Her heart swelled with gratitude for God's mysterious plans unfolding so perfectly. She and Caleb planned to live in the parsonage, her father would move in with Martha and Springer Smith had already taken over at the livery under Caleb's watchful eye, at least until the boy learned to handle the horses. Oh, how Springer's face had lit when Caleb had asked if he'd be willing.

Louisa Smith stepped off the church steps and headed up the street.

"She's coming," Annie said, her breath suddenly shallow and quick. She looked to her fellow brides. "Are we ready?"

Both ladies straightened and raised their chins as if marching into a parade. What an affair this wedding promised to be—better than any Saturday night dance Cañon City had ever seen.

"Here we go," Annie said as she opened the door and set the bell to ringing.

"Like I always say—" Martha linked her arm with Hannah and winked at Annie as they filed out to the boardwalk "—the more the merrier."

Annie fought the urge to hike her shimmering skirts and run to the church and into Caleb's arms. The effort consumed a good deal of her composure until they mounted the swept stairs and she peered through the doorway into the sanctuary.

Caleb stood at the head of the room in a new white shirt and borrowed frock coat, a string tie at his throat and a groom at each elbow.

His dark eyes locked on hers and drew her to the end of the terribly long aisle where she stopped before him, her heart in her throat. Their gaze broke when Robert moved to Hannah's side and Caleb looked away to officiate over the eager couple.

Annie's own bouquet quivered like Hannah's, but against the easy rhythm of Caleb's warm voice, her heartbeat soon settled and her mind wandered back over the past five months. She had dared to venture west with her father. And in the doing, she had found much more than she could have dreamed—a vast and magnificent land and a wealth of love far greater than all the gold in the Rocky Mountains.

And every ounce of it shone in the smile of the horse handler who now held out his hand to her.

"Annie?"

With a yearning in her breast at his mention of her name, she entwined her fingers in his and took her place beside him. The next great journey was about to begin.

The journey of her life as Mrs. Caleb Hutton.

* * * * *

REQUEST YOUR FREE BOOKS!

2 FREE INSPIRATIONAL NOVELS
PLUS 2
FREE
MYSTERY GIFTS

Love Inspired®

YES! Please send me 2 FREE Love Inspired® novels and my 2 FREE mystery gifts (gifts are worth about $10). After receiving them, if I don't wish to receive any more books, I can return the shipping statement marked "cancel." If I don't cancel, I will receive 6 brand-new novels every month and be billed just $4.74 per book in the U.S. or $5.24 per book in Canada. That's a savings of at least 21% off the cover price. It's quite a bargain! Shipping and handling is just 50¢ per book in the U.S. and 75¢ per book in Canada.* I understand that accepting the 2 free books and gifts places me under no obligation to buy anything. I can always return a shipment and cancel at any time. Even if I never buy another book, the two free books and gifts are mine to keep forever.

105/305 IDN F49N

Name _____ (PLEASE PRINT) _____

Address _____ Apt. #

City _____ State/Prov. _____ Zip/Postal Code

Signature (if under 18, a parent or guardian must sign)

Mail to the **Harlequin® Reader Service:**
IN U.S.A.: P.O. Box 1867, Buffalo, NY 14240-1867
IN CANADA: P.O. Box 609, Fort Erie, Ontario L2A 5X3

**Are you a subscriber to Love Inspired books
and want to receive the larger-print edition?
Call 1-800-873-8635 or visit www.ReaderService.com.**

* Terms and prices subject to change without notice. Prices do not include applicable taxes. Sales tax applicable in N.Y. Canadian residents will be charged applicable taxes. Offer not valid in Quebec. This offer is limited to one order per household. Not valid for current subscribers to Love Inspired books. All orders subject to credit approval. Credit or debit balances in a customer's account(s) may be offset by any other outstanding balance owed by or to the customer. Please allow 4 to 6 weeks for delivery. Offer available while quantities last.

Your Privacy—The Harlequin® Reader Service is committed to protecting your privacy. Our Privacy Policy is available online at www.ReaderService.com or upon request from the Harlequin Reader Service.
We make a portion of our mailing list available to reputable third parties that offer products we believe may interest you. If you prefer that we not exchange your name with third parties, or if you wish to clarify or modify your communication preferences, please visit us at www.ReaderService.com/consumerchoice or write to us at Harlequin Reader Service Preference Service, P.O. Box 9062, Buffalo, NY 14269. Include your complete name and address.

LIDIR13R

REQUEST YOUR FREE BOOKS!

2 FREE INSPIRATIONAL NOVELS
PLUS 2
FREE
MYSTERY GIFTS

Love Inspired

HISTORICAL
INSPIRATIONAL HISTORICAL ROMANCE

YES! Please send me 2 FREE Love Inspired® Historical novels and my 2 FREE mystery gifts (gifts are worth about $10). After receiving them, if I don't wish to receive any more books, I can return the shipping statement marked "cancel." If I don't cancel, I will receive 4 brand-new novels every month and be billed just $4.74 per book in the U.S. or $5.24 per book in Canada. That's a savings of at least 21% off the cover price. It's quite a bargain! Shipping and handling is just 50¢ per book in the U.S. and 75¢ per book in Canada.* I understand that accepting the 2 free books and gifts places me under no obligation to buy anything. I can always return a shipment and cancel at any time. Even if I never buy another book, the two free books and gifts are mine to keep forever.

102/302 IDN F5CY

Name _____ (PLEASE PRINT)

Address _____ Apt. #

City _____ State/Prov. _____ Zip/Postal Code

Signature (if under 18, a parent or guardian must sign)

Mail to the Harlequin® Reader Service:
IN U.S.A.: P.O. Box 1867, Buffalo, NY 14240-1867
IN CANADA: P.O. Box 609, Fort Erie, Ontario L2A 5X3

Want to try two free books from another series?
Call 1-800-873-8635 or visit www.ReaderService.com.

* Terms and prices subject to change without notice. Prices do not include applicable taxes. Sales tax applicable in N.Y. Canadian residents will be charged applicable taxes. Offer not valid in Quebec. This offer is limited to one order per household. Not valid for current subscribers to Love Inspired Historical books. All orders subject to credit approval. Credit or debit balances in a customer's account(s) may be offset by any other outstanding balance owed by or to the customer. Please allow 4 to 6 weeks for delivery. Offer available while quantities last.

Your Privacy—The Harlequin® Reader Service is committed to protecting your privacy. Our Privacy Policy is available online at www.ReaderService.com or upon request from the Harlequin Reader Service.

We make a portion of our mailing list available to reputable third parties that offer products we believe may interest you. If you prefer that we not exchange your name with third parties, or if you wish to clarify or modify your communication preferences, please visit us at www.ReaderService.com/consumerschoice or write to us at Harlequin Reader Service Preference Service, P.O. Box 9062, Buffalo, NY 14269. Include your complete name and address.

LIHDIR13R

ReaderService.com

Manage your account online!

- Review your order history
- Manage your payments
- Update your address

---

*We've designed
the Harlequin® Reader Service
website just for you.*

Enjoy all the features!

- Reader excerpts from any series
- Respond to mailings and
  special monthly offers
- Discover new series available to you
- Browse the Bonus Bucks catalog
- Share your feedback

Visit us at:

ReaderService.com

RS13